Guidelines for Spiritual Discernment

Discover the Key to Correctly
Perceiving and Relating to God and Man

By

Gary H. Patterson

Copyright © 2003 by Gary H. Patterson
gfsdbooks@netscape.net

Guidelines for Spiritual Discernment
by Gary H. Patterson

Printed in the United States of America

ISBN 1-591608-80-5

All rights reserved. No part of this publication may be reproduced in any form, except for brief quotes, without the written permission of the author. No altering of its content in any form is permitted.

Unless otherwise indicated, all Scripture quotations are from the New King James Version of the Bible. Copyright © 1994 by Thomas Nelson, Inc. The Holy Bible, New King James Version Copyright © 1982 by Thomas Nelson, Inc.

Unless otherwise indicated all definitions were either taken or adapted from Strong's Concordance definitions, Online Bible Millennium Edition 1.12.

Xulon Press
www.XulonPress.com

Xulon Press books are available in bookstores everywhere, and on the Web at www.XulonPress.com.

Dedication

I would like to dedicate this book to my darling wife, Teresa, for her support, encouragement, input, and whose sensitivity to the Holy Spirit has proven to be quite valuable throughout our adventures in Christ, and to my wonderful daughter, Grace, whose character is looking more like her name as I watch her grow up. I appreciate and love you both very much.

Special Acknowledgments

I am very grateful to my niece, April (Duvall) Krieger, for her time spent in proofreading this book. A big "thank you" also to Larry Trammell for his comments and time spent in proofreading this book, without whose critique, this book would only have been 120 pages long.

Endorsements

"... I have known Gary Patterson for some years, and I have always been impressed by his ability to listen, and then speak. I have also noticed that as he teaches, he brings forth the word of the Lord with a convicting edge. This can only come from someone who is quiet in God's presence, learning valuable lessons about not only listening, but carefully discerning when to speak—making the heart of the Father known, and bringing correction in trying circumstances. Gary is a discerning man. In *Guidelines for Spiritual Discernment*, Gary shares the heart of God for His people concerning careful discernment. The manuscript is frank, upfront, revealing, convicting, and addresses some fine keys in discerning truth from error as well as being able to become a discerning listener, prepared for times of counseling others. As an educator, I look for tools to teach others to know the heart of God better, and exploring the aspects of God's personality that so few Christians often recognize. I believe Gary Patterson has explored this area of our Father, and brought forth divine truths for the Body to examine as well as use."

Larry B. Reese
Author, President, Founder,
RAFFA Front-Line Ministries, Atlanta, Ga.

"I read the book, *Guidelines for Spiritual Discernment,* by Gary H. Patterson, and I found myself stopping and asking for forgiveness in the middle of the pages. I have come to realize, as never before, the importance of developing spiritual discernment. For example, there have been times in my life where I failed to correctly discern and was deceived. This happened because of things that I had read. I allowed my thinking to be conformed to the world through such influences. In addition, as a pastor, I am constantly examining myself to make sure I am leading the sheep instead of wrongly controlling them. I do not want to be a tool of deception in other people's lives either.

Most of us want truth, but many of us refuse to meditate on the written word to receive it. Instead, we would rather receive someone else's revelation rather than God's. Instead of being discerning, we allow ourselves to be led by our "heroes." This a tremendous book and if you read it, I believe you will be enlightened in the area of discernment and repent as I did."

Sam Fenceroy, pastor
Mt. Olive Church
Plano, Texas

"Today, there is a smorgasbord of options to expand ones God consciousness from Native American spirituality, Eastern mysticism, Western European paganism, shamanic medicine, techniques for achieving cosmic consciousness through various forms of yoga all with the promise of experiencing various avenues to spiritual enlightenment. In the Gospel of Luke, we read how Jesus challenges his listeners to discern the times.

He said to the crowd: "When you see a cloud rising in the west, immediately you say, 'It's going to rain,' and it does. And when the south wind blows, you say, 'It's going to be hot,' and it is. Hypocrites! You know how to interpret the appearance of the earth and the sky. How is it that you don't know how to interpret this present time?" Luke 12:54-56 (NIV)

In the apocalyptical books and chapters of the Bible, there are three reoccurring warnings. Apocalyptical literature refers to end times and the Second coming of Christ.

1. <u>Warning against deception.</u> What is so powerful about deception is that those who are deceived don't even realized they are deceived. Deception is powerful.
2. <u>Warning against false prophets.</u> According to scripture, people who are 80% right and 20% wrong are false prophets.
3. <u>Warning against false teachers.</u> One of the primary reasons many churches are empty today is because of false teachers.

The focus of apocalyptical literature is the need for believers to be watching and ready for the Second Coming of Christ. Gary Patterson's book contains biblical revelation and truth that can help to protect the believer from the deceptive satanic bacteria that is prevalent in today's society. In Matthew 24, Jesus warned the disciples three times against being deceived at the end of the age just before His return. May we all take heed of Christ's warning and be watchful and ready for His appearance."

Dennis Lindsay
President, CEO
Christ for the Nations Bible Institute
Dallas, Texas

Foreword

Part One

"*Guidelines for Spiritual Discernment* is a thought-provoking book that challenges our traditional thinking concerning traditional subjects. This is not casual reading and must be approached through the eyes of the Spirit.

The author is one of my spiritual sons and is very passionate about order in the life of the Church. He is also committed to seeing true revival expand throughout our nation and the nations of the world. Gary Patterson is a man of prayer with a servant's heart—a great combination. He also has a strong revelation gift.

Guidelines for Spiritual Discernment is on my recommended reading list. After 36 years of full-time ministry, I'm persuaded that discerning of spirits is the most coveted of the nine spiritual gifts.

As you read this book, you will benefit from Gary's many hours of research, study, and review. May you be blessed and edified as you receive additional insight, instruction, and correction concerning these foundational truths.

Let's restart the journey."

Dr. Dale Gentry
Breakout Prayer Network
Roswell, New Mexico

Part Two

A Personal Profile

I HAVE A TINGE OF REGRET as I write this foreword for *Guidelines For Spiritual Discernment.* For, even though this book contains some of Gary Patterson's deep, sometimes witty, always weighty wisdom and practical insights for living, many people on this side of eternity will never come to know him and his precious family intimately as I have.

Gary's life has the distinguishing mark of one who has genuinely encountered God and walks *with* Him instead of one who has merely gathered concepts and can therefore only talk *about* Him. Furthermore, although Gary often moves in the gifts of the Holy Spirit, what really stands out about him are the wonderful character qualities of the Lord that comprise "the fruit of the Spirit," listed in Galatians 5:22-23. This is important because, although the Lord Jesus highly esteems the gifts of His Holy Spirit, He places an even higher premium on the fruit of His Holy Spirit becoming evident in His children's lives.

Guidelines For Spiritual Discernment is an authoritative book that is full of living, Holy Spirit-birthed revelation instead of dead, religious interpretation. The reason Gary's words have spiritual impact and life is because he has "eaten" them in the crucible of God's dealings and because Gary has been willing to die to self.

Gary is a true "friend of the Bridegroom" who eagerly desires and labors to see the bride of Christ totally enraptured and in love with (and, therefore, obedient to) her promised Husband from Heaven—the Lord and Messiah Jesus. On numerous occasions, I have been present as Gary travailed to see a people raised up in the earth in whom Jesus can be revealed in holiness without hindrance or taint.

Numerous times, the Patterson's have opened their hearts and home to my wife and me, feeding us spiritually, emotionally, and physically, as they have also done for many others. We have been blessed to be able to pour out our hearts to them, confessing weaknesses, needs, and prayer requests. How insightful and loving they

Foreword

have been, often administering the power of the Spirit of God with prophetic insight, unction, loving care, and wisdom to the deepest parts of our beings. Probably some of the reasons God can use them so effectively as "spiritual sponges" to draw out and minister to issues in other hearts is because they love Him so and have such open hearts with very little spiritual and emotional "clutter" to impede His flow.

Even so, there are times when Gary has displayed humility and meekness by confessing his faults to me, just as God's people are instructed to do in James 5:16. I share this in the hope that you will derive comfort and encouragement knowing that this helpful, challenging book's author knows that he desperately needs God. However, because of this desperate and honest reaching out to God in prayer, Bible study, fellowship with other disciples of Jesus, and praise and worship, Gary is being transformed and is experiencing an increase of the kingdom of God within and around him.

Gary and I have prayed that God would use this book to enlighten you and spur you onward in a never-ending quest to be deeply in love with (and therefore obedient to) the Lord Jesus and to know Him intimately, please Him perfectly, and delight Him supremely.

Peace to you as you pursue the Lord and Messiah Jesus—the Prince of Peace—and as you constantly adhere to His *Guidelines For Spiritual Discernment.*

John 14:21 (Amplified Version),

Larry Trammell,
Ablaze Ministries
www.ablazeministries.com
USA—770.476.0230 (ext.2)

Contents

Introduction xix

Part One

The Inherent Safeguard 25
The Weapon of Deception 29
The Dependability of the Anointing 33
Discernment and Authority Structure 35

Part Two

Exercising Your Spiritual Senses 47
Characteristics of the Light 51
Developing Spiritual Discernment 57
The Daily Workout 59

Part Three

Judging by Appearance 71
To Compare or Not to Compare 73
Natural Reactions 79
Familiarity and Unbelief 83
Personal Likes, Dislikes, Fears, and Insecurities 97

Self-righteousness 101
Some Other Important Issues 107

Part Four

Correct Biblical Interpretation 113
In Whom Do You Boast? 115
Recognizing Persuasive Words 119

Part Five

Seeing God with a Pure Heart 143
Discernment: An Extension of Love 145
Grace and Truth 149

Part Six

Some Final Guidelines on Discernment 155
Words for the Wise 157
The Conclusion 165

Introduction

A spiritual revolution is beginning in the Church that will challenge our understanding of New Covenant church life. This revolution will involve a shift from an old rigid paradigm of church structure to a "new wineskin" that can contain, preserve, and strategically advance what God desires to pour out in this final hour. This paradigm shift will necessitate the need for purer hearts, relationships, spiritual visions, and discernment in the Church. Although one of the purposes for this book is to help give biblical insight as to where God desires to take the Church over the next few years, the application of its content is timeless.

The main purpose for this book is to instill within you, the reader, an excellent spirit in the way you relate to fellow believers, spiritual leaders in the Church, those you oversee, and the Lord. This will largely depend on your cultivating an enduring love for the truth and on how you see or discern through your spiritual eyes. If there are not major advances in these areas in the Church, we will disqualify ourselves from being fit for the Master's use in the last days.

Throughout the course of this book, you will see that purity of heart is the criteria for developing spiritual discernment, and that your ability to discern God and your fellow man correctly will keep you from deception in this final hour.

It is not my intent to deal with discernment in its role as one of the nine gifts of the Spirit even though there may be some unavoidable overlapping between the two. The gift of discerning of spirits (1 Corinthians 12) is vital to effective Christian ministry. The gift is not developed, but received, and is available to both the mature and immature. Spiritual discernment must be exercised daily in order for us to mature in Christ. "But solid food belongs to those who are of full age, that is, those who *by reason of use* have their *senses exercised* to *discern* both good and evil" (Hebrews 5:14; italics mine).

Neither is it my intent to give you information about people, ministries, or organizations that might be suspect of error or heresy. Instead of attempting to define all of the details of darkness, we will search out the depths of God's ways. My intent is to stir and help develop within you the ability to recognize God in a crowd—a crowd of many other voices and manifestations that may or may not *appear* to be like His.

This is not a book of formulas that, when applied, will cause a person to develop spiritual discernment. Neither is it, essentially, a "how to" book. Its main purpose is to reveal the Lord's ways concerning spiritual discernment so that we can learn how to cooperate with Him in its development and approve of the excellent things (Philippians 1:10). This includes interpreting Scripture and experiences in a manner that is excellent in the Lord's eyes. While I do address some controversial doctrinal and experiential issues in the body of Christ, my sole purpose is to help you develop spiritual discernment.

The main purpose for the questions in the "Truths in Review" section at the end of each part is for you to test your ability to spiritually comprehend the truth contained therein. I would encourage you reread the part if you have a problem answering the questions. The questions could also be used for group discussion. By the time you finish this book, you should see a marked difference in your spiritual sensitivity to the Lord and other people.

While reading this book, I would encourage you to get your Bible out and be prepared to look up Scripture. You are commanded by the Lord to: "Be diligent to present yourself approved to God, a worker who does not need to be ashamed, rightly dividing the word of truth" (1 Timothy 2:15). After reading this book, you may be convicted of being a worker who should be ashamed accordingly. If so, just thank God you are no longer deceived and set your heart to love the truth as the Lord commands.

This book was written for those who hunger for righteousness—whose greatest ambition is to be like the Lord Jesus. May your life be profoundly changed so that you will be presented holy and blameless before Christ when He returns to gather us unto Himself.

Spiritual discernment, according to the Biblical standard, is the ability to see a person, spirit, or thing as they are from God's perspective. This entails distinguishing them from the way they appear outwardly. Since the devil's ministers have the ability to *appear* as an angel of light (2 Corinthians 11:14), there must be an inherent safeguard for the Christian. The Apostle Paul points out in that same context (vs. 3, 4), that because of this deception, it would be possible for the Christian to receive *another* Jesus, spirit, and gospel. He feared that they would be deceived as Eve was by the serpent. Therefore, the answer is obvious as to whether we, as Christians, can be deceived. More importantly, God's remedy to keep us from it is spiritual discernment.

> "My son, if you receive my words, and treasure my commands within you, (2) so that you incline your ear to wisdom, and apply your heart to understanding; (3) yes, if you cry out for discernment, and lift up your voice for understanding, (4) if you seek her as silver, and search for her as for hidden treasures; (5) then you will understand the fear of the LORD, and find the knowledge of God".
> (Proverbs 2:1-5)

Part One

(Please read *Introduction* to book first)

The Inherent Safeguard

Within every Christian is an inherent safeguard that leads them in the way of truth and warns them when subjected to deceptive influences. This safeguard is identified in Romans 8:16:

"The Spirit Himself bears witness with our spirit that we are children of God."

It is by the witness (testimony) of the Holy Spirit in our spirit that we know we belong to God. Likewise, we have an internal witness of the Spirit that causes us to know God. This involves being able to discern what is not of Him—the true from the false, good from evil, and the genuine from the counterfeit.

The Apostle John said it this way:

> "But the anointing which you have received from Him abides in you, and you do not need that anyone teach you; but as the same anointing teaches you concerning all things, and is true, and is not a lie, and just as it has taught you, you will abide in Him".
>
> (1 John 2:27)

The main reason why Christians are deceived is their failure to develop and be taught by this anointing. This inward witness or anointing and its development is the key to our growing up in Christ.

Geese are known for their ability to return before winter to warmer climates in the south. They have a God-given internal homing device that takes them back to the same place (home) each year. There is an old saying that is appropriate: "Home is where the heart is." Jesus proclaimed also: "...Where your treasure is, there your heart will be also" (Matthew 6:21). As a compass always points toward the north, even so the inherent witness of the Spirit in our hearts points toward Him who is the Way, the Truth, and the Life. He is our Home and Treasure. If we will listen to the inherent witness of the Spirit in us, we will never miss God's perfect will. We will understand that this world is not our home, and all that it offers will not be appealing to us. Our hearts will be locked in to the coordinates of our destiny in Christ—of becoming like Him.

Notice that 1 John 2:27 states that we would not need any man to teach us. What does he mean by this? No person or thing, whether pastors, priests, preachers, or religious organizations can take the place of your personal relationship with the Father. Neither can anyone, except Christ, mediate that relationship. We must learn to follow our internal homing device. It is the primary means we have to know the Father.

Our relationship with God cannot depend solely on a person or church and the teachings thereof. Furthermore, if we depend on someone else's discernment or teaching to protect us from the devil's deception, then we are already deceived. In varying degrees, this deception dominates the Church because of our failure to understand that no man or organization can monopolize the truth. God's New Covenant design leaves no room for such to take place.

One of the most important things that an airplane pilot must learn is how to read and fly solely by the airplane's instruments. It was speculated that the reason John F. Kennedy Jr. became the untimely fatality of an airplane crash was because of his inexperience in flying an airplane solely by its instruments. An inability to read and follow an airplanes guidance instruments could result in the pilot thinking that he is ascending when he is actually descending. While pilots must trust and follow the instructions of air traffic controllers, thus preventing disaster, their onboard instruments are their closest friends. They are with them wherever they go. In a similar way, the Christian must learn to follow their internal guidance instrument—the witness of the Spirit. The Holy Spirit is their closest friend and is always with him or her. The Christian must also trust and follow the "air traffic controllers" assigned to them in order to make it safely to their destiny. The "air traffic controllers" represent the body of Christ.

There are three promises that frame the New Covenant as defined in Hebrews 8:10-12.

They are:

1. <u>Sanctification and Relationship</u>: "I will put My laws in their mind and write them on their hearts; and I will be their God, and they shall be My people"
(v.10)

2. <u>A thriving and unmediated relationship with God</u>: "None of them shall teach his neighbor, and none his brother, saying, 'Know the LORD,' for all shall know Me, from the least of them to the greatest of them"
(v.11)

3. <u>Forgiveness and cleansing from sin</u>: "For I will be merciful to their unrighteousness, and their sins and their lawless deeds I will remember no more"
(v.12)

Most of us are familiar with and understand the first and third promise, but what about the second? In the Old Testament, Moses went up the mountain and received God's revelation for the people. He spoke with God face to face (Numbers 12:8; Deuteronomy 34:10), and was actually living out a New Covenant promise under the Old Covenant. Why then do we, as New Covenant people, live under Old Covenant restrictions? In the Old Covenant, the people were not allowed to even touch the mountain for fear of their lives (Hebrews 12:18-20). Now, we are conditioned in varying degrees by man-made religious traditions to not "go up the mountain" for ourselves. Listen to what Jesus declared:

"The law and the prophets were until John. Since that time the kingdom of God has been preached, and EVERYONE is pressing into it" (Luke 16:16; emphasis mine).

We cannot send a "Moses" up the mountain to receive the revelation of God for us. We are *all* commanded to press in.

CHAPTER ONE

The Weapon of Deception

*E*veryone, from the least of us to the greatest, can know God, and this is His deepest longing toward humanity. His indwelling Spirit is the securer of the fulfillment of that promise in every believer. What God seeks to secure is as a precious treasure to which He has given us a map. However, we have tossed aside our map and compass and have listened to other voices besides our Father's. In seeking to please men instead of God, we have created a religious system that makes people dependant on it instead of Him. We have become like geese that refuse to listen to their homing devices, and, as the result, have lost our way home—to our Treasure.

The children of Israel were comfortable with staying away from mountain Sinai—the mountain that could not be touched—but Moses was not. The reason for this was the hardness of their hearts. Their spiritual eyes were veiled (2 Corinthians 3). Moses had an unveiled heart that could see beyond the animal sacrifices to the Lamb of God who would take away the sin of the world. For this reason, he was able to draw near and enter the fiery presence of God.

Beloved of God, are you comfortable with staying where you are? Are you convinced there is far more to Christianity than having your needs met and being "successful" or blessed? If we are rich in faith toward God, the resulting inward contentment and security will prove to be enough for us in this life. How many churches have put up more "blockades" to God's people experiencing His fullness than "road signs" to show them the way? What are we substituting for the fire and glory of God's presence in the meeting place?

Has the pulpit in varying degrees become the "high place" in the Church? For example, how many of us are convinced that in order to know the Lord, that we must go through someone standing behind a pulpit? You might respond, "Well, I don't believe that." But do you act like it? How many of us make the pulpit and platform the focus of the corporate church meeting and not the presence of the Lord? The main purpose for the apostles, prophets, evangelists, pastors, and teachers is to direct the people into a thriving and unmediated face-to-face relationship with the Holy One of Israel. If the fivefold ministry does otherwise, they are misusing their God-given authority. *Woe be unto us if we attempt to compete with God for the affections of His people.* God's design in the New Covenant requires us to remove every stumblingblock out of the path that leads to an individual face-to-face relationship with Him. We must rediscover the map and the compass to this lost treasure that is so dear to God's heart. Let us throw off the beliefs of men, and we will *if* we truly long for the Lord with *all* of our heart. Only then can we function as the united and many-membered body of Christ.

There is a God-given order in 1 Corinthians 12-14 that plays a major role in removing such stumblingblocks. These passages of Scripture make it clear that one member of the Church is not more important than another—*from the least to the greatest.* While a spiritual leader's function is different and responsibility greater, they are still servants to the body as are the rest of the members (Romans 12:6; Ephesians 4:7).

Having been conditioned to depend on a religious system or empire, how many of God's people do not know they are being cheated from experiencing this much neglected New Covenant promise (knowing Him face-to-face without mediation or outside influence)? *Any church structure that does not facilitate the fulfillment of this promise in the lives of every believer does not originate from God.* In some cases, religious pharaohs, who are disguised as preachers, are more interested in using people to build their kingdom (ministry) instead of using their place of influence to build people. Oh, how we have become accustomed to a lie, and have learned to prefer dependency on gifted ministers to sonship with the Father.

What is a main weapon of deception the enemy uses against God's people? To get them to replace a total dependency on the inherent witness of the Spirit with teaching from someone else. What is the purpose for teaching in the Church then? Mainly, to train and equip believers for the work of the ministry (Ephesians 4:11). This entails giving definition and bringing to maturity what has been deposited within the people by the Lord and to cause them to become entirely dependent on the Spirit's witness or anointing within them. This anointing, without exception, is entirely trustworthy and dependable, as John declared "...and is true, and is not a lie." By becoming entirely dependent on the anointing within them, the child of God will become an entirely dependable *asset* to the body of Christ.

CHAPTER TWO

The Dependability of the Anointing

During one service in a church I used to attend, my attention was drawn to a man who was serving on staff at that time. When I saw him, I knew in my spirit that something was not right. Afterward, my spirit was troubled every time I saw him. (Notice that I did not say that my emotions were troubled. We can know the difference between troubled emotions and a troubled spirit. If our spirit is troubled, we will sense it from deep within where the Holy Spirit dwells.) Within one year this man had resigned his staff position, was arrested by the police, found guilty, and put in prison for crimes he had committed. The Spirit was bearing witness in my spirit the whole time that this man was living a lie, but I could not put my finger on the problem. If I had diligently sought the Lord concerning the issue, this man could have possibly been confronted long before his arrest. I learned something very important from this experience: *The anointing within me does not lie, and I need to completely trust it. Someone's life, including mine, may depend on it.*

We were sitting on the porch at a couple's home who are very dear to us. They had asked us to come and pray specifically for the wife concerning physical problems that she was having. As she was talking about an experience she had with another relative, I sensed a knot well up in my throat and was nearly overcome by feelings of rejection. At the time, I did not completely understand what was going on, but after conveying what was happening with me, we petitioned the Lord. She confirmed that there was hurt in her heart concerning the relative. I had sensed hurt and rejection in her that neither she nor her husband knew was there.

There have also been a number of occasions, while sitting in a church service or watching Christian television, that I have sensed the teacher or preacher step over from speaking by godly revelation into a spirit of error. We can know the difference between those things that come from God and the product of a person's own understanding. The inherent witness of the Spirit has kept me from such error on many occasions. The Holy Spirit never lies and surpasses all human understanding.

John also pointed out in 1 John 2:27 that we abide in Christ by the teaching of the anointing within us. All outside teaching must agree with its teaching, and it will always agree with Scripture and the corporate witness of the Spirit (not opinions or speculations) in the body of Christ. *The cause for much of the instability in Christian's lives today is that they are taught more from an outside influence rather than from within.* This will result in an inability to abide in Christ and in our being tossed back and forth like the waves of the sea when tested.

While teaching from outside sources can be dependable, especially from mature and spiritually healthy leaders, it may not be on every occasion. Thank God that we have an anointing that will keep us safely in Christ if we will heed its instructions. The anointing will be our immovable anchor and link to God during our sojourn on earth. Do *you* believe it is entirely dependable? Notice that I did not ask if you had complete confidence in your ability to hear from God. If we are going to clearly hear from God, we must first have complete confidence in the dependability of the Holy Spirit within us. If we are confident of this, then confidence in our ability to hear from God will not be a problem.

CHAPTER THREE

Discernment and Authority Structure

If we are submissive to authority then we will walk in Kingdom authority in the earth (see Jesus' encounter with the Roman centurion in Matthew 8:5-13). How we relate to authority will also affect our discernment, and this will, consequently, affect our spiritual growth. While the witness of the Spirit is inherent in the individual Christian from the new birth, we must remember that we are only one member of a many-membered body. We need the rest of the body of Christ, and they need us (not like we need Christ as our Head), so we must submit to one another in the fear of the Lord (Ephesians 5:21). Our being rightly connected to the body solely depends on our primary connection to the Head—Jesus— "...From Whom the whole body, joined and knit together by what every joint supplies, according to the effective working by which every part does its share, causes growth of the body for the edifying of itself in love" (Ephesians 4:16).

As we draw life from Jesus, our connection to His body will be a source of edification for the other members. We will then benefit from their connection to us. If we are not first rightly connected to our Head then we will not experience true body life. Submission to Jesus our Head is the prerequisite to our being rightly aligned to the body of Christ, and, consequently, submission on any level will not be a problem for us. However, it is possible to submit to (have as a "covering") Christian organizations, churches, ministries, and ministers and still not be rightly connected to the Head. Problems with various types of immorality in the Church do not stem from a lack of submission to a human "covering," but stems from a lack of true submission to the Head—Jesus.

Our connection to the body of Christ is primarily not for our benefit but for the benefit of the rest of the body. Furthermore, our relationship and submission to the body plays a vital role in determining our spiritual growth or maturity. This is because the rest of the body judges, validates, and refines our input. As the result, we benefit and grow because our discerning abilities are sharpened.

The Role of Servant-Leaders

The previous reference to "the rest of the body" includes the mature apostles, prophets, evangelists, pastors, and teachers. We must correctly understand what their role is in the body of Christ before we can truly benefit from their input. How we perceive them will determine how we receive from and relate to them. In varying degrees, the body of Christ, either esteems their spiritual leaders too much or sometimes not enough. This can be in part attributed to the way we have structured our corporate church meetings but it is mostly attributed to a horrific lack of true discipleship.

What can happen is that a spiritual leader is deemed in the hearts of the people as the greatest member among the brethren. The greater portion of the responsibility of keeping this from happening falls on the shoulders of the spiritual leader, but because of immaturity, woundedness, and pride in the leader, it does happen. The people are conditioned to look to him or her instead of the Lord. When the spiritual leader fails to produce the expected spiritual "high" or spiritual food, the people begin to complain and become disgruntled. The spiritual leader then loses favor with the people, and begins to blame the people for various problems in the church. Complaints begin to arise from the leadership concerning the people and from the people concerning the leadership. In some cases, the spiritual leader will end up leaving

Discernment and Authority Structure

the fellowship or there will arise another leader in their midst who leads half of the people away to start another church. The irony of all this is that, in the beginning, the spiritual leader could do no wrong in the eyes of the members. Now, however, they want a new "king."

The only spiritual "covering" in the Kingdom of God that a person can truly claim is the *only* Head of the Church—Jesus Christ. He covers us with His feathers and under His wings, we take refuge (Psalm 91). This is the Biblical chain of command: from Jesus—the Head—to each individual member of the body of Christ. There is no military chain of command between each individual member of the Church and their Head—Jesus (i.e., from Jesus, to the pastor, and then to the lay members). Each member, however, must respect and obey the authority of Christ their Head when expressed through a spiritual leader. The purpose for the fivefold ministry is to oversee and help bring to maturity each individual member's unmediated relationship and submission to the Head. They are to aid the members in staying under their true Covering and Commander in Chief.

To claim a spiritual leader, organization, or a Church body as our "covering" is similar to saying that a human being, group, or organization is our best safeguard against deception or harm. We already know the best safeguard against deception. It is the Teacher who lives in each one of us. Of course, I am not saying that being part of a local Church body does not provide, to a certain degree, a covering protection over our lives. The body of Christ defines this protection, mainly the mature leaders, by fulfilling its role as overseers of each member's submission to their true Covering. We do benefit from being rightly connected to the body of Christ as long as the body and its leaders are in correct relationship with one another.

Again, I emphasize: when we are rightly connected to Christ, then, and only then, will we experience true body life and all its benefits. Then there will be true submission to one another in the fear of the Lord. Each member will be able to discern the proper role of spiritual leaders in the Church and know how to rightly relate and submit to them.

The Purpose of True Spiritual Authority and Rule.

The role of New Covenant spiritual leaders is not to exercise authority OVER the people, but is to serve them according to the grace given to each leader for ministry. Jesus made it clear in Matthew 20:25-26 that the authority structure in the Kingdom of God is not like that of the world.

"But Jesus called them to Himself and said, 'you know that the rulers of the Gentiles lord it *over* them, and those who are great exercise authority *over* them. (26) Yet it shall not be so among you; but whoever desires to become great among you, let him be your servant'" (italics mine).

Jesus makes it clear that we are to exercise authority OVER demons, sickness, and disease (the works of the devil) in Luke 10:19, Mark 16:17-18, and 1 John 3:8. The role or function of leaders in the Kingdom of God toward other people is that of a servant.

We are BUILT UPON the FOUNDATION of the apostles and prophets, and Jesus Christ is the Chief Cornerstone (Ephesians 2:19-22). The authority given by God to any spiritual leader in the Church is not for ruling over the people as a king but is for overseeing as a shepherd. True Kingdom authority is the foundation that edifies, upholds, and serves the rest of the body. It is not for ruling OVER people. For this reason, the only true spiritual covering one can claim in God's Kingdom is Jesus Christ. This holds true whether you are a man or woman.

There is neither male nor female in Christ (Galatians 3:28). The Lord has used women just as powerfully and effectively to preach, prophesy, teach, and disciple others as men. Only within the confines of the marriage covenant is a man the head of a woman (1 Corinthians 11:3). Even a man's headship over his wife is not like that of a king over his kingdom. In the Kingdom of God, Jesus is her Head. She is accountable to Christ first, and then to her husband. Christ has preeminence over all. Every individual, both men and women, will stand alone before Christ on Judgment Day and give an account for their stewardship in this life. There will be men who will suffer great loss on that Day because of putting stumblingblocks in the way of women fulfilling their destiny in the

Kingdom of God. There will be women who will receive great reward for enduring and overcoming those stumblingblocks.

True spiritual authority and leadership in the Kingdom is proven within the institution of the family as revealed in 1 Timothy 3:1-13. Verse 5 states "If a man does not know how to rule his own house, how will he take care of the church of God?" The home is the proving ground also for the woman. If a woman aspires to be a teacher or desires a place of leadership in the Church, she must first prove her maturity (honor, respect, meekness, responsibility) in the home (1 Peter 3:1-6). Her submission to Christ is proven by her submission to and respect for her husband. Those who are not married, both genders, must prove their submission to Christ by submitting to their parents. Any passage of Scripture that would appear to put down women and their role in the Kingdom of God must be interpreted in light of this. Women are in no way inferior to a man in the Kingdom of God because God is not partial to anyone, but He is partial to faith. If a woman has faith in God to do what He intends and the man does not, then God will honor the woman over the man.

It is helpful to understand that obedience to human authority (whether delegated or usurped) is relative but submission is absolute. Peter and John were very submissive, proven by their respectfulness to the Jews who beat them for preaching in Jesus' name (see Acts 5). However, they did not obey the demands of the Jews to stop doing it, thus making their obedience relative as to whether or not it infringes on their obedience to Christ. They had a submissive attitude toward all, but they feared God and not men.

We must show the utmost respect for and be submissive to ALL authority in spite of whether or not they are of good character. Of course, that does not mean that we obey everything that the authority demands of us, because our obedience to Christ takes precedence over all. For example, if a woman believes she is married to a jerk, that does not give her the right to be disrespectful or withholding toward him in any way. (It is easier for any man to become a "jerk" if his wife constantly shows disrespect toward him.) If the husband places demands on her that violates conscience or infringes on her obedience to Christ, then she must respectfully, with a submissive and meek spirit, communicate that to her husband. He will then be able to recognize the Spirit of Christ in her and will be more apt to soften his heart. This does not mean that she will be kept from suffering for righteousness' sake.

It is interesting to note the definitions and use of the Greek words translated "rule" in the New Testament.

1. <u>Christ's rule</u>: "And He Himself will *rule* them with a rod of iron. He Himself treads the winepress of the fierceness and wrath of Almighty God" (The Revelation 19:15 and also see 12:5; italics mine). The primary definition of the Greek word "poimaino" used in this case is "to feed, tend a flock, keep sheep." Then it is defined "to govern or rule." This word is actually translated "feed" six times and "rule" four times in the New Testament (AV - Authorized Version). In this, we see Jesus revealed as the Great Shepherd King. Even in wrath, the Lord's shepherd heart is revealed. He would gather all people unto Himself if they would listen and submit (Matthew 23:37). Jesus' ruling authority is foundational to our understanding all rule or authority in the Kingdom of God.

2. <u>A man's rule in his house</u>: "If a man does not know how to *rule* his own house, how will he take care of the church of God?" (1 Timothy 3:5; italics mine), and <u>an elder's rule in the Church</u>: "Let the elders who *rule* well be counted worthy of double honor..." (1 Timothy 5:17; italics mine). The primary definition of the Greek word "proistemi" used in these cases is "to set or place before." Then it is defined "to set over" and can be translated "to be a protector or guardian, to give aid to, care for, give attention to." The word is translated "rule" five times, "maintain" two times, and "be over" once in the New Testament (AV). One can see in these definitions a picture of a shepherd *over*seeing or looking after the welfare of the sheep. This is what is intended by the definition "be over," and flows in harmony with Christ's teaching.

3. "Those who rule over you:" This phrase is used three times and only in the book of Hebrews (13:7, 17, 24), and is referring to leaders or ruling elders in the Church. The primary definition of the Greek word "hegeomai" used in these cases is "to lead." Then it is defined "to go before, to be a leader." It is also defined as "to have authority over" as a king, prince, viceroy, and such. The use of the word "over" in the phrase "those who rule over you" is an unfortunate translation. It is not included in the Greek text. According to Strong's Concordance, only one Greek word is translated "over you" in the passages of Hebrews. It is never translated this way anywhere else in the New Testament. It is almost always translated "you" or "your." In this context, "over" is only used when "rule" and "you" are used together. While this Greek word for "rule" can be used to describe a "chain of command" type authority, the best translation of these passages, which harmonizes with Christ's teaching, is "those who rule or lead you."

4. Chain of command: There is another Greek word, "arche," that is used to define a "chain of command" type rule or authority. Its primary definition is "beginning, origin." Then it is defined "the person or thing that commences, the first person or thing in a series, the leader." It is translated "beginning" forty times and "principality" eight times in the New Testament (AV). It is only found in reference to the authority structures of the world, of angels, and of the kingdom of darkness. *It is never used in reference to the authority structure in the Church or family.*

Understand that unless we, as God's people, have a proper grasp of authority structure in the Church (and family), we will not spiritually mature in the manner that the Lord intends. Because many of us have been conditioned to accept an authority structure that debilitates our spiritual growth, it necessitates that we rightly discern the proper role of the Church and its leaders. We are in dire need of reformation in the Church. Why do you think so many of God's people never leave the carnal or baby stage of Christianity and go on to maturity? Why are so many living their Christian lives always focusing on their needs instead of having a heart of a servant? It would be far better for the Church and her leaders to embrace reform now than to endure shame and irrevocable loss at the judgment seat of Christ.

In conclusion, mature spiritual leaders are the main catalysts used by God to mature the body of Christ. Unless we understand their proper role and heed their words, our spiritual growth will suffer greatly. Their authority is designed by God to help us deal with any tendencies we may have toward pride, rebellion, offense, unteachableness, rejection, apathy, complacency, divisiveness, idolizing or wrongly relating to those in authority (civil or spiritual), and selfish ambition as revealed in coveting positions of authority and attempting to draw life (self-worth, acceptance, a sense of superiority) from our God-given gifts and positions or functions. Mature spiritual leaders can also be used to proclaim and release God's judgment in the Church as revealed when the Apostle Peter judged Ananias and Sapphira in Acts 5. Above all, mature ministers in the body are to set the example of true service and humility. Their influence primarily and effectively works toward helping us maintain our connection to the Head and depending on the inherent witness of His Spirit in our hearts as we function in the body of Christ and the world.

Precious Father, I thank you so much for true fathers in the body of Christ. Lord, do raise up more so that spiritual abortion would cease in the Church. Father, bring correction and discipline into our lives according to Your perfect will through whoever you wish. Help us to see every member of the body of Christ as you do. Jesus, we desire to abide in You every moment. Amen.

> "A man who isolates himself seeks his own desire; he rages against wise judgment".
>
> (Proverbs 18:1)

Prophecy:

"There is a design against which the gates of hell cannot prevail. It comes out of that which is born within your hearts by My Father. It is written and it is conceived. The law and the prophets testified to My coming as Immanuel—as the Word that was made flesh. This reality was conceived in the heart of Peter when I asked, "Who do you say that I am?" He did not know that because a man had taught him, and neither did he come to that conclusion by searching the Scriptures. No, My Father revealed it to him. Peter understood that the Scriptures testified of the Messiah who was to come, but He knew Me because My Father revealed it. What was revealed to Him confirmed what was already revealed many years before and recorded in Scripture. Revelation is the rock upon which I have built My Church. Though all of hell gathers against her, she will not be moved or prevailed against as long as she continues on this rock.

I am calling My Church to return to this rock and to cease replicating what originates from men. It is wood, hay, and stubble and will not endure the Day of the Lord. You are precious ones—living stones being built together by Me that I may be your God and You may be My people. You are either working against Me or with Me. I am working to fashion you after My image and not that of flesh and blood. You will be my finished product that will glorify My Father and not man. Give your heart to no other, for only of Him, to Him, and through Him are all things, and in the end, I will rejoice over you as My masterpiece. Behold, I stand at the door and knock. Beloved, keep yourselves from idols."

Truths in Review

1. What is the main purpose or goal intended by this book? (See the *Introduction* for questions 1 & 2)
2. What is the biblical definition of spiritual discernment and what does it entail?
3. What is the Christian's greatest and most effective weapon against deception?

Guidelines for Spiritual Discernment

4. What is a main reason why Christians become deceived?
5. It is acceptable to do something contrary to the teachings of Christ, even if we are convinced that we have heard from God. True or False? Why or why not?
6. What is the main cause of instability in Christian's lives?
7. Our maturing in Christ depends on the development of what in our lives?
8. Who are the main catalysts God uses to help us develop this in our lives?
9. Are women equal to men in the Kingdom of God? If so, then how does this affect the way we interpret Scripture passages that would *appear* to portray her as less than men? If not, give scriptural references.
10. Spiritual leaders are to mediate our relationship with God? True or False? Why or why not?
11. Spiritual leaders can be compared to generals in the armed forces. In the Kingdom of God, they are the chain of command above us. True or False? Why or why not?
12. What two verses of Scripture in the New Testament clearly teach that the individual believer does not need anyone to teach them, and promises that they will know the Lord from the least to the greatest?
13. These two verses teach that we do not need relationships with anyone else in the body of Christ. True or False? Why or why not?

Part Two

Exercising Your Spiritual Senses

In Matthew 24, Jesus indicated that deceptive influences would increase in the earth before His return, and the Apostle John stated, "...the whole world lies under the sway of the wicked one"(1 John 5:19). He also revealed:

> "For all that is of the world – the lust of the flesh, the lust of the eyes, and the pride of life—is not of the Father but is of the world. And the world is passing away, and the lusts of it; but he who does the will of God abides forever".
>
> (1 John 2:17)

In other words, we, as Christians, will have many opportunities while living in the world to develop our discerning ability, and it is imperative that we do so. This development will involve our reckoning dead the sinful flesh within us that these influences may expose. Doing this is essential if we are going to reap the full benefit of the fellowship we have with the Lord and the saints. That fellowship can only be maintained as we continue in Christ's love by putting to death everything of self-centeredness. The Lord's ultimate goal is that we would be clear channels of His love, with spiritual discernment as an extension of it.

The wicked one's influence in the earth is summed up in the lust of the flesh (evil desires and uncontrolled bodily desires), the lust of the eyes (coveting and having cravings for or lusting after what our eyes see), and the pride of life (boasting in others, our accomplishments, and ourselves). These motivating forces are not always recognized by the way they appear outwardly. They usually are hidden behind what would seem to be sound logic, but are actually cloaked in twisted "truth" and "reasonable" lies that slander God's character and subvert His ways. The serpent tempted Eve with a fruit that looked delicious and would give knowledge and spiritual exaltation beyond what God was "allowing" her. By twisting God's words, he deceived Eve into questioning what God commanded. He made what was forbidden look wonderful and made the One who forbade them to eat of that tree look bad. You know the rest of the story.

These fleshly motivating forces can be hidden under cloaks of religious form, good works, "sincerity," charisma, flattery, false humility, and such. A person may be impressive, godly in appearance, successful, have superior intellectual ability and outward splendor, many talents, and even operate in the gifts of the Spirit, but inwardly be bound by bitterness. Possibly, their "…house is the way to hell, descending to the chambers of death" (Proverbs 7:27). They could be whitewashed tombs that are full of dead men's bones and uncleanness as Jesus declared concerning the scribes and Pharisees of His day (Matthew 23:27). They honored God with their lips but their hearts were far from Him (Matthew 15:8).

> "And this is the condemnation, that the light has come into the world, and men loved darkness rather than light, because their deeds were evil. For everyone practicing evil hates the light and does not come to the light, lest his deeds should be exposed".
> (John 3:19-20)

The Lord commands us to walk as children of light and not fellowship with the unfruitful works of darkness. We are to expose or reprove them (Ephesians 5:1-17). The light exposes and displaces the works of darkness, and we will do likewise as we walk in the light. Yet, we must be alert because the father of lies will attempt to get us to dabble in and become accustomed to the "shadows" by tempting us to compromise morality. The enemy subtly coerces us day-by-day and week-by-week to compromise a little here and a little there—to play in the shadows. The result is that our spirit becomes desensitized to the things of the Spirit of God, and to the Kingdom dynamics of grace and faith. We slowly forget what manner of person we are, and our conscience becomes increasingly callused or like a mirror that is losing its ability to reflect (James 1:23-25). Consequently, it becomes much easier to be motivated by fleshly lusts and pride.

It is quite obvious that the enemy is attempting to desensitize the children and youth of our nation to the Spirit of God and sensitize them (as if it is normal or acceptable) to unholy spirits of the New Age movement, white and black magic, witchcraft, and the occult through various media. Some of these things *appear* to be innocent, but are actually wolves in sheep's clothing or, better yet, "Trojan horses." One reason the Lord told Joshua to meditate in His word day and night was to prevent him from being desensitized by the darkness (Joshua 1:8). We will become like that with which we occupy our minds. Parents, what mostly occupies you and your children's minds?

> "See then that you walk circumspectly [exactly, accurately, diligently], not as fools but as wise, redeeming the time, because the days are evil".
>
> (Ephesians 5:15)

The Lord requires us to walk diligently, exactly, and accurately in the light and not stray off the path into the shadows. By doing so, we will know "...what is acceptable [well pleasing] to the Lord" (v.10).

> "But if we walk in the light as He is in the light, we will have fellowship with one another, and the blood of Jesus Christ His Son cleanses us from all sin".
>
> (1 John 1:7)

We are called to walk in the light as God is in the light. There is no darkness in Him. He alone is the standard and the source of life for all things.

CHAPTER FOUR

Characteristics of the Light

In 1 John 1:6, John equates walking in the light with practicing the truth. He implies that if we are not practicing the truth (light), we are practicing deception (darkness). Darkness entails the self-deception of believing that we have fellowship with God while not practicing the truth. Thus, although walking in darkness, a Christian can appear to be walking in the light. The fellowship that is formed in darkness would then be the counterfeit of true Christian fellowship as defined in 1 John 1:7. Those who operate in this counterfeit fellowship will unite with others in darkness and seek to tear down, through faultfinding, those who are walking in the light.

The devil is the father, originator, and perfecter of lies. He abides and thrives in darkness or deception. That which is conceived in a counterfeit fellowship is therefore a lie, *even if it is based on fact*. It will always be hostile to the truth and is hostile to our fellowship with one another and the Lord. *Even truth without love can have its roots in darkness or deception.*

To illustrate the point, Matthew 12:1-14 points out that the religious leaders during that time accused Jesus and His disciples of breaking the Sabbath. Their accusations against them were based on *fact*: Jesus' disciples did go through the grain field, pluck grain, and eat it, and He did heal people on the Sabbath. Contrary to the accusations, keeping the Sabbath was a truth that Jesus totally embraced.

Guidelines for Spiritual Discernment

The religious leaders' accusations were obviously rooted in deception. They were absolutely convinced that Jesus and His disciples were in error, when they were themselves void of love, true justice, and mercy. Jesus told them that since they would have no reservations about pulling one of their sheep from a pit on the Sabbath, then they should not have a problem with helping a person in need, knowing that people are more valuable than sheep.

The nature of those who walk in darkness is to use facts mixed with twisted truth to intimidate or condemn in some way those who walk in the light. For fear of being proved wrong, they do not want those whom they have accused to succeed or prove in any way to have God's favor. The light is a threat to the false security of those who walk in darkness. Pride is the false covering that gives such people a false sense of security. Consequently, it prevents them from coming and submitting to the light. Pride will cause someone to judge the light as being darkness. That is how deceptive it is.

Ironically, the religious leaders during that time accused John the Baptist, who came neither eating or drinking, of having a demon, and then they accused Jesus, who came eating and drinking, of being a drunkard, glutton, and a friend of tax collectors and sinners (Matthew 11:18-19). Those who walk in darkness will always prove to be more devoted to condemning what is a threat to their false security than they are to the truth. You will never be able to please them because they become obsessed with destroying the credibility of those who are a threat to their self-made image.

In one church with which we were involved, I was straightforward with the pastor concerning my eschatological views being different from what he teaches. Having been given a place of influence in the church through teaching, preaching, prophesying, and such, I considered it necessary to inform him concerning my views and assure him that I would not influence the people toward them. In spite of this, suspicions and faultfinding arose for various reasons but not because I was influencing the people toward my views. While the suspicions were linked to fact, they were conceived in darkness. The Lord opened my spiritual eyes, and I saw a vicious looking evil spirit. It had a dagger in its hand and was saying, "This is my territory, and don't you dare intrude!" This spirit of Jezebel had been given a place of preeminence in that fellowship. Let us be careful that what we call "discernment" is not suspicions that have been conceived in darkness, and, consequently, give the devil a dwelling place among us.

> "He who loves his brother abides in the light, and there is no cause for stumbling in him".
> (1 John 2:10)

To practice the truth is to love others as the Lord commands. Where there is no such love, there exists only darkness and many causes for stumbling. This "stumbling" includes faultfinding, backbiting, gossip, slander, unrighteous judgments, jealousy, suspicion, flattery, competitiveness, territorialism, and ungodly control and manipulation. It inevitably becomes diabolical in influence.

> "But he who is spiritual judges all things, yet he himself is rightly judged by no one".
> (1 Corinthians 2:15)

The spiritual are not those who merely teach or claim to have the truth, but are those who *practice* the truth by loving others. Those who practice the truth are an indictment against those who pretend to do so. They are not moved by the fleshly judgment of others and are confident that their works will withstand the Day of Judgment.

Late one evening, I was sitting in front of my computer, working on this book, and suddenly the presence of God came on me in a profound way. Afterward, I sensed such a hatred and repugnancy to even look at the darkness or spiritual nakedness in other people. This was not mixed with a self-righteous attitude, but it came with a sense of wanting to cover the sin, shame, and weaknesses of others.

What if you were standing on a busy street corner in a major city, and a gang of people came and grabbed you, tore off all of your clothes, and left you naked for all eyes to see? To add insult to injury, suppose they began to yell as loud as they could in an attempt to parade your nakedness to all passing by. Some of the bystanders would look and laugh at the shame of your nakedness and some would even be indifferent toward your plight. In your overwhelming embarrassment, you would scramble for any cover you could find. Yet, all you would need is *one true friend* who would help cover you. In a similar way, we all fit into the category of the gang, the bystanders, or the friend in relation to other people, and we all know what it is like to be victimized in varying degrees. All of us would rather be among the bystanders, but when we place ourselves in the shoes of the victim, things take on a different light. "Do unto others as you would have them do unto you" carries new and relevant meaning.

If we walk in the light, we will seek to cover the spiritual nakedness of others through the blood of Christ. This defines how we can be a spiritual covering for one another. Those who love the light will likewise hate the darkness of sin because of what it does to people, not because of a self-righteous and condescending attitude. *Those who hide behind self-righteousness do not truly know the righteousness that is of faith in Christ—a faith that works by divine love* (Galatians 5:6). Sin has left us without spiritual clothing or without right standing before God, but we can rejoice along with Isaiah the prophet: "I will greatly rejoice in the LORD, my soul shall be joyful in my God; for He has clothed me with the garments of salvation, He has covered me with the robe of righteousness..." (Isaiah 61:10). We do not, like Adam and Eve, need to seek out our own fig leaves. Jesus has become our covering.

Here are some characteristics of those who walk in the light:

1. They are teachable because of their awareness of God's love.
2. They are unhypocritical. They do not appear to be some thing they are not.
3. Their faith is in God and not in their ability to point out what is wrong in others. Those who parade another person's failure or use it as a means to control them are walking in darkness. It is proof that they are not exercising faith toward God in their behalf and are void of love.

4. They will not attack or tear down another person's character but will seek to edify, exhort, and comfort them. They will bring correction with love when necessary.
5. They dare not seek to bring attention in any way to the darkness they see in their brother. If they do, it is solely for bringing them into a place of faith in God for deliverance. They cover their brother's spiritual nakedness with love.
6. Their disposition toward the darkness in their brother is the same as the testimony of the blood of Christ toward them.
7. They have a strong immovable confidence in the power of the light and its ability to expose the works of darkness and rightly deal with it. Therefore, they will not seek to find fault with their brother.
8. They know the light is not a thing, but is a Person—Jesus Christ, and will, therefore, understand that the light is His love revealed in deed and in truth.

Something very significant happened during the controversy surrounding the Presidential elections of 2000 A.D. and the vote count in Florida. An individual arose and began, through demagoguery, to influence a certain ethnic group in this nation. The result of his influence could have been very tumultuous. As I was praying for this individual, the Lord spoke to me and said that He was going to judge him. Not long after that, it was aired over the major television networks that he had been involved in an adulterous affair. As the result, this man's bewitching influence over the people was broken, and the tide of outrage subsided. I did not rejoice over this man's plight, in fact, I prayed that the Lord would have mercy on him after knowing he was going to be judged. Thank God, as far as I know, there was not much attention given to it by those whom he politically opposes.

God can use us in this manner, if we will allow him to deal with anything in us that would gloat in the exposure and failure of others, especially those we would consider to be opponents to our particular cause or even those who oppose the Lord's will.

One cannot walk correctly without being able to see clearly. If we are not walking in the light, then our perspective is not compatible with the truth, God's love, the blood of Christ, and the Holy Spirit no matter how convincing or how much factual evidence that we think we have against a person. The light is not against us. If we are of the light then we will not be wrongly against others. We will not be like the gang of people who exposed the nakedness of a person and then paraded it and will not be like those who laughed or were indifferent either. We will live in harmony with the love that covers a multitude of sin. Of course, we are to confront those who are deceived. It is possible to make someone's fault a point of discussion and not sin against them in the process. This is done by our making sure that we are not deceived and walking in darkness (Ephesians 5:11; Matthew 7:1-5).

Only in His light are we made pure;
Only in His light will our spiritual sight be sure.
As we look into His holiness,
Our sins we will confess.
In hope we will be kept,
Even as by His mercies we are swept.
Secured by His power through faith,
Enraptured by His amazing grace.
This will be our only desire,
That we may endure His purging fire.
Then, in His Day, without shame or reproach,
we will be found,
When we hear the Lord's trumpet sound.

CHAPTER FIVE

Developing Spiritual Discernment

"But solid food belongs to those who are of full age, that is, those who by reason of use have their senses exercised to discern both good and evil".

(Hebrews 5:14).

In the above passage, the writer of the book of Hebrews was addressing an issue of slothful immaturity among the Jewish believers of that day. They had become "dull of hearing" (v.11). According to God's time clock, they should have matured to the level of being teachers—those who help ground people in God's truth—and not that of needing to be taught again foundational principles or "milk" (v.12). When weighed in the balance they had been found wanting.

Now look at verse 13:
"For everyone that partakes only of milk is unskilled in the word of righteousness, for he is a babe."

The term "unskilled" is defined *"inexperienced in."* Having been taught by the first apostles, the Hebrew Christians had excellent opportunities to become experienced in the word of righteousness (or the word that results in or brings righteousness). However, they allowed their hunger, passion, and love for the truth to slip away

(Hebrews 2:1). When these ingredients are missing, the door is opened for slothfulness. This then dulls our ability to hear God. *Our ability to hear or distinguish God determines our ability to discern both good and evil.* The writer's use of "good and evil" in this context would include morality, doctrine, and spirits, whether they are human, evil, angelic, or divine.

The term *discern* used in our text is defined as *"a distinguishing, discerning, perceiving, recognizing, judging"* (these five definitions will be used interchangeably throughout this book). The word "use" indicates something that has become a habit. Therefore, we can determine from the writer that a habitual ability to distinguish between good or evil (bad) fruit, doctrine, or spirits defines spiritual maturity. These three things determine how one affects or influences other people's lives. We are either operating in a God-ordained means of influence over other people or a counterfeit.

The writer of the book of Hebrews painted a word picture of an athlete who must get into a daily discipline of exercise in order to win the prize. Accordingly, we must exercise our spiritual senses to maintain the stamina needed to overcome in this life and receive the prize at Jesus' return. We overcome by keeping ourselves pure—by walking in love. Exercise is not necessarily fun—it is work and requires *effort* on our part. Yet, it pays off when the strength gained through it is put to the test. The ultimate reward of exercise is winning the prize. Let us press toward the goal.

CHAPTER SIX

The Daily Workout

What does it mean to exercise our spiritual senses? This begins with learning to hear the voice of God on a daily basis. As I said earlier, if you are dull of hearing, you will be dull in your discernment. *If you can discern your Father in Heaven, you can discern anything, whether it is good or evil.* If we have learned to recognize His voice in our personal lives, then we will know Him when He reveals Himself through others. We will also know when it is not Him. If we cannot recognize God's voice, we will not be able to grasp His love either. Keeping ourselves in the love of God is contingent on knowing His voice (Jude 1:20-21), and Jesus said that His sheep know His voice and the voice of stranger they will not follow (John 10:3-5).

Why then do Christians still get deceived into following other voices? If we are not acquainted enough with the genuine, we can be deceived by the counterfeit. So, we must discipline ourselves to become acquainted with the Lord and His ways daily. Just as an athlete must exercise daily to qualify and compete to win the prize, even so we need godly routines that will train us to overcome in all areas.

My wife would know my voice even if she was unaware of my presence. This is because of her having become so acquainted with it every day for a number of years. Likewise, we must be able to recognize the Lord's voice without being aware of His presence or even in the midst of many other voices. This requires our giving Him our undivided attention. The more time we spend in true communion with the Lord, the stronger and sharper our spiritual senses become.

My daughter went through a lesson some time ago in knowing the voice of her Father in Heaven. One day she told her mother that the devil had been telling her that she was fat. Those of you who know her, know that this is far from the truth. I sat down and began to talk with her about how to respond when such thoughts go through her head. The Lord had me approach it from the angle of there being another voice that was trying to seduce and bring her under the control of another father—the father of lies. So, instead of telling those lying voices "No, I am not fat," we decided to instruct my daughter to say, "I will only listen to the voice of my Father in Heaven and another I will not follow." This was an important lesson for her in recognizing the Lord's voice from other voices and on how to deal with it. In this case, listening to such voices could be the beginning stages of anorexia or bulimia. The proper training will produce the desired results.

Those who live according to the Spirit set their mind on the things of the Spirit (Romans 8:5). Notice that *we* are required to "set" our minds on the things of the Spirit. In other words, we must make sure our mind is in harmony with the mind of the Holy Spirit. Our responsibility is to direct our thoughts, emotions, desires, and wills toward Him. This involves our absolutely abandoning ourselves to the things and ways of the Spirit of God on a daily basis. The development of our spiritual senses involves our allowing the fruit of self-control to restrain anything that would keep us from setting our mind on the things of the Spirit. The result will be a keen ability to hear the voice of our Father.

Thank you Father for the fruit of self-control (temperance). I surrender completely to its influence in my life. By it, I can freely exercise my will, subdue my desires, and calm my emotions in order to focus on the things of the Spirit. I thank you that, according to Romans 8:9, I am not in the flesh but in the Spirit because the Spirit of God dwells in me. By walking in the Spirit, I overcome everything of the flesh, sin, the devil, and the world. Help me to understand that I do not overcome the flesh first in order to walk in the Spirit; that I only overcome by virtue of the indwelling Spirit of God. Amen.

Becoming Acquainted with the Genuine

In order to hear the voice of God, one must value what He has to say. As mentioned earlier, this involves a hunger, passion, or love for the truth. We purify our hearts and souls by obeying the truth, and the pure in heart will see God (1 Peter 1:22; Matthew 5:8). This "seeing" is the ability to discern or distinguish Him and His voice from other counterfeit influences. If our hearts are pure then we will recognize Him who is pure. In order to recognize evil, one must become completely acquainted with the good.

> "But we all, with unveiled face, beholding as in a mirror the glory of the Lord, are being transformed into the same image from glory to glory, just as by the Spirit of the Lord".
> (2 Corinthians 3:18)

Our lives are transformed and discerning ability sharpened by our being occupied with the Author of all that is good, and not by being preoccupied with the bad. If you want to keep from being deceived, then intimately know Him who is the Truth.

In 2 Thessalonians 2:9-12, Paul states that those who do not receive the love of the truth will be given over to strong delusion. The point here is that if we do not love the truth, we will end up loving a lie. In consequence, it would make it very difficult for us to come to the knowledge of the truth in spite of an ever-increasing accumulation of information (2 Timothy 3:7). Without a love for the truth, we will lack the purity of heart necessary to see Him who is pure Truth, and will be susceptible to deception. A person who has not spent a lot of time in becoming acquainted with real one hundred dollar bills could easily be deceived by a good counterfeit. Without having knowledge of what is true, one has no point of reference by which to recognize the counterfeit. This is the main reason why Paul commanded that novices not be given a place of leadership in the Church (1 Timothy 3:6). Because they are not acquainted enough with humility, they could become puffed up with the pride of the devil. Such pride will bring condemnation (God's judgment) on them.

Now let us look at some practical guidelines for spiritual discernment.

The Importance of Childlikeness

We were sitting in our living room giving premarital counseling to a young couple and something very enlightening took place. The young man had been struggling with jealousy and possessiveness in their relationship. At one point, I noticed that he was looking around everywhere as if to see something. I asked him what he was doing, and he said that the Lord wanted to show him something. I responded, "Look with your spiritual eyes and not with your natural eyes." Afterward, the Lord revealed to him that instead of needing his fiancé's love, that he needed His love. The young man conveyed that he believed that he already knew this; however, he realized that he had not truly known this truth in a manner that would set him free.

It became clearer to me through this experience of what Jesus meant when he spoke of becoming as babes or children before the Lord. We can say we believe something but not be convinced in our heart of it to the point that it sets us free. Believing is truly seeing and submitting to the truth and how it applies to specific areas of our heart. Even demons believe that there is one God and tremble at the thought (James 2:19), yet it does them no good because of their dreadful lack of humility or childlikeness. They are entirely given over to pride. If a person truly believes, then they will receive the substance of their faith—God's provision.

The Lord has "...hidden these things [truth] from the wise and the prudent and have revealed them to babes [untaught, unskilled, unclever, undiscerning[i]]" (Matthew 11:25). "Let no one deceive himself. If any one among you seems to be wise [taught, skilled, clever, discerning[ii]] in this age, let him become a fool that he may become wise" (1 Corinthians 3:18). We are nothing apart from God. All genuine truth, revelation, and discernment come only from Him. We cannot understand Scripture or the true nature of things (including our heart) unless He reveals it to us. It is impossible to grasp genuine truth or an understanding of the things of God by our mental processes. "But the natural man [those who depend on their own understanding] does not receive the things of the Spirit of God, for they are foolishness to him; nor can he know them, because they are spiritually discerned" (1 Corinthians 2:14). As helpless babes, we must throw off everything that bears the aroma of pride or self-sufficiency, and then present ourselves to God for our daily bread.

Meditating in the Written Word

In order to maintain a love for the truth, one must habitually meditate in the written word of God. This is in harmony with the inward witness of the Spirit and should be the main way the Lord speaks to us. There have been numerous occasions where the Lord has poured out revelation through Scripture that has washed my mind and lifted me up to newer heights in Him. These times with the Lord have been a major stabilizing influence in my life. *Do not ever forget that your ability to discern will be directly proportional to your ability to hear or recognize God.*

Correct methods of interpreting Scripture are crucial to spiritual discernment. (In using the word "interpreting," I am not referring to our trying to figure it out.) *What you believe will affect how you perceive.* The witness of the Spirit or the anointing is the primary method God has given His people to discern good from evil. The development of this ability is largely dependent on our sitting at the feet of our Beloved and meditating in His word. It is only by the anointing within us that we can understand Scripture, and the Spirit will use our understanding of it to instruct us in the way of truth as opposed to error. Yet, He will only use that of which He has given us understanding, and not our misinterpretations and misapplications of it. The word of God is the *sword of the Spirit* (Ephesians 6:17). It is to be wielded as *He* desires and not according to our thinking.

Guidelines for Spiritual Discernment

The first method of interpreting Scripture, which can never be violated, is that it must be in harmony with the original intent of the Holy Spirit. Secondly, we must understand that there are some things that the Holy Spirit never does. For instance, He never glorifies flesh, only Christ, and He will not contradict Himself. The Spirit and Holy Writ will always agree. There is also spiritual common sense that is needed in understanding Scripture. I will deal with this in more detail in another chapter.

Some of what people call "revelation" is only a product of their biased or influenced deductive reasoning. Does God use the reasoning ability of people? Yes, but only after it has been purified by foundational truth. True meditation does not involve making our minds passive as in the Eastern religions. A passive mind opens the door for demonic influence and oppression. Christian meditation involves our focusing our thoughts on the Lord, what He has done for us and others, and the written word. A mind focused on Him in this way aids our spirit in receiving revelation from Him. Our minds then benefit from the understanding of the revelation. Biblical interpretation does involve thinking on our part, but our thinking cannot violate the spiritual common sense that is established in our understanding through foundational truth, knowledge, and facts. Truth is needed for character and to prevent error, knowledge and facts are needed for accuracy and because of our ignorance and potential for deception. If our thinking is contrary to these, it will be difficult, if not impossible, for us to correctly understand Scripture.

The Greeks were known for their great oratory skill. They produced philosophers like Plato, Socrates, and Aristotle. These were considered by some to be the greatest among the thinkers, but, according to their writings, they never attained the knowledge of the true God. The reason for this was that true God-given revelation was not the foundation for their philosophy (their philosophy was the product of their deductive reasoning). Knowledge and their ability to achieve it was their god. This is why Paul stated that the message of the cross was foolishness to the Greeks (1 Corinthians 1). Only people with a childlike heart will be able to receive truth from God—people who know they do not have the ability to figure it out.

We must have a foundation of truth established in our hearts that keeps our thinking in check or keeps us from being puffed up in our minds as were the Greek philosophers. This foundation serves as a spiritual compass that keeps our reasoning ability on course. It stabilizes our thinking and is the most important expression of Christian character. It consists of humility and meekness, and these two virtues define childlikeness. These virtues form the compass that will keep us on course in properly understanding Scripture. If our words do not diffuse the aroma of the One who is meek and lowly in heart, then we are under the wrong "yoke" and are speaking from ourselves (see Matthew 11:25-30). We are still blind even though we think that we see.

Jesus proclaimed: "He who speaks from himself seeks his own glory; but He who seeks the glory of the One who sent Him is true, and no unrighteousness is in Him" (John 7:18). The Greek philosophers sought their own glory by speaking from their deductive reasoning. Their words contained no humility or meekness. We must make sure that our spiritual compass is working in interpreting Scripture or we will be deceived, be drawn to the praise of men, attempt to still God's glory, and eventually bring judgment own ourselves.

Worship and Listen

We must worship God with a listening posture. We should spend more time listening to our Father than talking to Him. Would you want someone to take up all your time telling you what he or she has to say, and not value what you have to say? We must quiet our souls before the Lord in order to recognize the still small voice.

Praying in the Spirit

We must build ourselves up, habitually exercising our faith by praying in the Holy Spirit (this involves praying in tongues with the interpretation), and thus keep ourselves in the love of God (Jude 1:20, 21). This will place us into a flow of God's revelation that will strengthen our spirits, subdue our souls, and bring our bodies into subjection. It is necessary to press in daily until God's life and love is flowing through us. This is learning to abide in Him who is the Truth. "He who believes in Me, as the Scripture has said, out of his heart will flow rivers of living water" (John 7:38). "But they that wait upon the LORD shall renew their strength; they shall mount up with wings as eagles; they shall run, and not be weary; and they shall walk, and not faint" (Isaiah 40:31).

Fasting Food

Last (but not least), fasting from food often will help keep our spiritual vision sharp. Living in this world can be defiling and dull our spiritual senses. Fasting will help to silence the voice of the flesh, thus making us more sensitive to the Lord's.

Father, enable me to listen to and obey Your voice continually and in any given situation. Show me the true state of my heart. I have no skill, cleverness, or understanding that can deliver me or impress You enough and cause you to act in my behalf. I empty myself of any tendency to get people to look to me instead of You and of making a reputation for myself. I become as a fool so that I can be wise. Oh, dear Lord, I do not want to be one of those from whom You hide things. Open my eyes, in Jesus' name. Amen.

Truths in Review

1. What are the three main motivating forces in the world? These also sum up the wicked one's influence in the world.
2. Is it necessary for us to overcome these in our spiritual walk so that our discerning ability can be developed? Why or why not?
3. Can a Christian be deceived by the devil and, if so, what does he use to deceive them?
4. Are the works of the devil always easily discerned? Why or why not?

5. Is it OK for Christians to dabble in moral "shadows?" How does this affect one's sensitivity to the Holy Spirit?
6. Name three characteristics of those who walk in the light.
7. What does it mean to be spiritually naked? Can you remember a time in your life when you were in such a vulnerable state?
8. We are never to expose the darkness in another person. True or False? Why or why not? If we are, then how?
9. Where in the Bible is being mature in Christ ("of full age") equated with those who have developed their spiritual senses to discern both good and evil?
10. What role does Scripture play in developing our discernment?
11. If you can discern your Father in Heaven, you can discern anything, whether it is good or evil. True or False? Why or why not?
12. In order to discern and deal with the works of darkness, we should spend a lot of our time reading books on other religions and the occult, watching a lot of television, conversing with demons, and fellowshipping with people who do not know Christ. True or False? Why or why not?
13. What role does childlikeness play in developing spiritual discernment?
14. Name other ways in which we can develop our discernment.

Notes

i. Information contain in these brackets were adapted from The Amplified Bible, Expanded Edition. Copyright © 1987 by the Zondervan Corporation and the Lockman Foundation, All Rights Reserved.
ii. Ibid

Part Three

Judging by Appearance

Throughout Scripture, there is a common thread that forbids judging things according to outward appearance. If we judge by appearance, we could be deceived by the things that appear to be of God but are not and condemn those things that appear not to be of God but actually are.

Over the past decade, there has been an increase in signs, wonders, and manifestations in the Church—mostly in Charismatic/Pentecostal churches, but not limited to that. There have been books written for and against such. Some spiritual leaders, from pulpits, radio talk shows, and other media, have openly condemned some of the manifestations, while others fully embrace the phenomena associated with what some have called "Renewal." Many believe it is the beginning of the last great outpouring of God's Spirit before Jesus returns. Among those who embrace the phenomena, there are testimonies of those who have had lives, marriages, churches, and ministries changed in varying degrees.

Paul rebuked the Galatians (3:1) for allowing certain teachers to sway their thinking away from the Gospel: "O foolish Galatians! Who has bewitched you that you should not obey the truth, before whose eyes Jesus Christ was clearly portrayed among you as crucified?" It is evident from this passage that Christians can be deceived into placing faith in something else besides Christ. Therefore, in all things, we must be alert to the bewitching influence of the devil. However, that does not give us the right to go on a "witch hunt." This means we cannot "burn everyone at the stake" who embraces teaching or phenomena that exceeds or *seems to* contradict our beliefs or experience.

We must correctly discern apart from the influence that spiritual leaders have over us, because their influence *may be* biased and not in harmony with the Spirit of truth. Many say that "everyone has the right to an opinion," but not before God. He commands us to judge righteously and not according to our thinking. We could end up unwittingly fighting against God if we are not careful. We must be as equally careful to correctly discern and not to wrongly judge others as we are careful about error.

In order to develop true spiritual discernment, the obstacle of judging things by appearance must be overcome. There are strongholds of mistaken beliefs that form the structure of judging by appearance. These are defined as follows:

1. Making judgments based on similarity in comparison
2. Our natural way of reacting to certain things
3. Familiarity and unbelief
4. Our personal likes and dislikes
5. Our fears and insecurities
6. Self-righteousness
7. Other Issues

Now, let us look at these structures of rationale and take them apart with the truth…

CHAPTER SEVEN

To Compare or Not to Compare

Some ministers have condemned what has been called "holy laughter" because the New Age people also have their version of it. Is this true spiritual discernment? Just because it violates our dignified version of Christianity—what we call decently and in order—and agitates us does not make it of the flesh or demonic. *If we are subjected to two separate incidences that look the same outwardly, that does not mean that the motive or spirit behind them is the same.*

There are similarities between other religions (including cults and the occult) and Christianity in method, truth, worship, signs, wonders, and manifestations. For example, witches speak in a demonic version of tongues, Muslims believe in one God, and Buddhist monks make sounds in worship similar to some Charismatic worship services. Also, remember that the Egyptian sorcerers were able to duplicate the plagues brought upon their nation through Moses up to a certain point. All of these examples have obvious similarities in appearance to things that are truly of God, but major differences in motivation and source.

> "We know that we are of God, and the whole world lies under the sway of the wicked one".
>
> (1 John 5:19)

The devil is a counterfeiter. The Spirit of truth glorifies Jesus (John 16:13-14). We can stand with the full assurance of knowing the spirit in which we are operating. For example, I have seen people attempt to cast a demon out of someone because of a particular manifestation. The problem was that the manifestation was of the Holy Spirit. How do I know? Well, I was the person on whom they attempted the deliverance. I was under a heavy anointing from the Holy Spirit at that time. This person was judging the situation by comparing it to a similar experience he or she had with demonic manifestations. This is not the way to determine whether someone is demonized. People have shaken under demonic influence and, yet there are those who have shaken in a similar manner under the power of God.

To further illustrate, let's say that two people, named Roy and George, have come to me for ministry because of having problems with anger. While ministering to Roy, I discern the presence of a spirit of anger. Now, just because his anger problem involves a demon, does that mean that the same would apply to George? Can we safely assume that all anger problems are demonic? No, because assumption is not a part of true discernment. In fact, the Bible does not support any such view. Neither does it teach that deliverance from the demonic is a "cure all."

Even though Roy may get set free from a spirit of anger, he still has to deal with anger as a work of the flesh. Anger is primarily a work of the flesh according to Galatians 5 and is not a just an evil spirit. Spirits of anger can inhabit that area of sin in our lives but they are not the sin (Ephesians 4:27). The Bible is clear as to how we are to discern the presence of a demon—by the gift of discerning of spirits—and not by assuming that every sin problem is or involves a demon.

True discernment has nothing to do with our comparing one incident with another because of outward similarities, and, consequently, condemning or approving it.

Samuel's Learning Experience

The prophet Samuel was told to anoint one of the sons of Jesse the Bethlehemite as king in place of Saul (1 Samuel 16:1). Samuel, in his natural understanding, was obviously looking for someone *comparable* to Saul who was taller than anyone else from his shoulders upward (1 Samuel 9:2, 10:23). In the midst of this event, the Lord gave Samuel an awesome revelation in reference to Eliab, the first of the sons to come before him:

> "Do not look at his appearance or at his physical stature, because I have refused him. For the LORD does not see as man sees; for man looks at the *outward appearance*, but the LORD looks at the heart".
>
> (1 Samuel 16:7; italics mine)

The Lord set the standard by which Samuel was to determine who was to be king of Israel. He corrected any tendencies Samuel had that would cause him to judge wrongly in the matter by delivered him from a tendency to discern by outward *comparison* and from being swayed by the partiality that Jesse had toward certain sons. After that, Samuel knew in his spirit, as they came before him, that none of the other six were the one either. *It would have been very difficult for Samuel to distinguish who was and who was not the one God had chosen without the standard being set and the necessary corrections being made.*

When David, who was the least likely choice of his father Jesse, stood before him, Samuel heard the Lord say that he was the one. *It is easy to hear God's voice when the other voices we have been entertaining are condemned and silenced.* We must petition God to do for us what He did for Samuel, and then we will develop true discernment. Judging by appearance is of the flesh. We have to see things as God sees them.

Is our discernment influenced by outwardly imposed standards to which we have conformed, but, nevertheless, are contrary to God's ways? Such standards take form in and find expression through ethnic culture, religious tradition, and various philosophies and beliefs common to particular groups of people. Principalities, powers, rulers of darkness, and wicked spirits influence the masses through such things. Like Samuel, we must identify the standard that we are using to judge others lest we end up resisting the Holy Spirit and become a tool of the devil.

What if you saw a sign, wonder, or manifestation that was not similar to those that are recorded in the Bible? The following is an interesting scenario. Let us see if we can determine what is true discernment.

Is it in the Bible?

One evangelist went to a large city, held evangelistic meetings for weeks, and could not get backing from various churches. Some reputable pastors in that city told their congregations not to go to his meetings. He had phenomenal success in spite of this. A large number of people made commitments to Christ. (Note that I do not know all the details of the events of this incident, but what I am presenting to you is true.)

One of the reasons why certain pastors told their congregations not to go to the meetings was that the manifestations common to this evangelist's meetings were not in the Bible. Is this a method that the Bible promotes to prove the validity of something or someone? Can all of God be fit into the confines of Scripture? The moral boundaries and doctrinal foundations are clearly laid out in Scripture, but what about the boundaries for signs, wonders, manifestations, and miracles? If there is nothing similar in the Bible to use for *comparison* and test such things should we automatically condemn them? If something is not in the Bible, a safe rule for determining its validity would be that it must be consistent with the character of God. However, there are things that the Lord required some people to do in the Bible that had THE APPEARANCE OF being inconsistent with His character.

For example, the Gospels tell of two instances where Jesus used spit to heal people. What if these events were not recorded in Scripture and the Lord directed me to do that today? Would I be marked as a false prophet? Many things Jesus did were not written about in the Bible. In fact, John said that he supposed that all the books in the world could not contain the record of them all (John 21: 25). The Holy Spirit can do whatever He wants to do, how ever He wants to do it, and use whatever means He chooses to accomplish it. He does not need or ask for our counsel. What He does will be consistent with His character, but not necessarily consistent with our perception of His character.

One must carry the pastors' conclusion concerning this evangelist further. If the manifestations are not of God, then the evangelist, at least part of the time, is operating in a spirit that is not of God. The only way one could have such power or influence over other people is through another spiritual power source. If he is operating in a spirit that is not of God, then he will produce fruit consistent with that spirit. I have judged this ministry according to Matthew 7:15-20. It states that you can know the true nature of a person by their fruits. A good tree cannot produce evil fruit and vice versa. This evangelist is obviously a good tree. Many testimonies have come forth of lives having been changed through his ministry. Equally as important, I have never been troubled in my spirit when around him, and he is a man that rules his house well. The Spirit of God bears witness with my spirit that he is of the truth. Furthermore, he has passed these same tests with thousands of others who have attended his meetings.

We cannot judge ministries by whether or not the signs, wonders, etc. associated with their meetings are in the Bible. This is not biblical. Are we supposed to be led by the Bible or by the Spirit of God? We can make the Bible say what we want, but try that with the Spirit of God! For example, the Jews said that Scripture did not speak of a prophet coming from Galilee, and they condemned Jesus on that basis (John 7:45-52). The irony of it all is that Scripture is clear in reference to the birthplace of the Messiah (Micah 5:2), and they did not even attempt to find out where Jesus was born. This is because that their hearts were already hardened toward Him, and they did not want to believe the truth.

> "For as many as are led by the Spirit of God, these are the sons of God".
>
> (Romans 8:14)

The sons of God are those who walk with Kingdom authority in the earth. We walk with this authority in the earth only when the Holy

Spirit leads us and not because we are trying to follow the Bible with our own understanding. The word of God is the sword of the Spirit (Ephesians 6:17). This is applicable whether it is spoken or written. God's word in any form has no authority unless wielded by the Holy Spirit. As we submit to the indwelling Holy Spirit, the Bible will have its proper place of authority and influence in and through our lives. We will fulfill Scripture as Jesus did when He walked on earth.

Telling God's people not to attend such meetings because the manifestations are not in the Bible is using their devotion to the Bible as a means to manipulate and control them. Of course, this does not necessarily mean that this was done knowingly or with deliberate intent, nevertheless, it does defy New Covenant order. *There is a big difference between guarding the sheep and controlling them.* We saw earlier what the best safeguard is that we have against deception, and *it does not come in human form.* A pastor or any other minister must encourage the people they oversee to use and develop the anointing that abides within them and test the fruit in such cases. It never fails. Spiritual leaders should always make sure that they are not teaching people to depend on their "expertise" at interpreting Scripture rather than depending on the inherent anointing that never lies or is mistaken. People can be mistaken or deceived, but the Holy Spirit is always true.

Could it be that God has sent such signs, wonders, and manifestations to the Church to break the control that certain church leaders have over God's people, and to get the people rightly connected to the only true Head of the Church? God sent Moses to Egypt with signs and wonders to set His people free then. Have we forgotten that ministry positions are not about controlling the sheep in accordance with what we *think* is right? It is about overseeing the acts of the Holy Spirit through them and laying our lives down for them in harmony with the mind of Christ.

So, who is right in this matter: the evangelist or the pastors? The witness of the Spirit in *every* believer is always right!

Father, as you did with Samuel, grace us with an ability to look beyond outward appearances and to know Your ways and the true state of things. We eagerly wait upon You. You are so wonderful! Amen.

CHAPTER EIGHT

Natural Reactions

What if you came across a man who was running around naked (or at least in his *Fruit of the Looms*), and when asked why he was doing it he replied, "The Lord told me to do this as a prophetic sign to a nation." What would be your *natural reaction* to such a person? Personally, my initial reaction would be to say that the man is insane and needs to be locked up for indecent exposure. Almost every believer would condemn it as being of the devil. Again, this would only be judging the matter by outward appearance and my natural reaction to him. It would be very easy to do so in such a case. That is why I chose this scenario.

Some of us would try to cast a demon out of him. Our rationale might be: "Didn't Jesus cast a demon out of a Gadarene man who was running around naked?"

Yes, but also recall that Isaiah the prophet was told by God to walk around naked for three years as a sign against Egypt and Ethiopia (Isaiah 20:1-6). This is proof that you cannot judge a matter or person by outward appearance. While this incident does bear the appearance of being inconsistent with God's character, yet, He did orchestrate it. Isaiah the prophet was naked, in his right mind, and doing the will of God, and, on the other hand, the Gadarene man was naked, a lunatic, and demon possessed. (Understand that I am not advocating obscenity in the Church any more than Scripture does. I am merely promoting true discernment.)

Can you imagine taking mud made from your own spit and rubbing it in someone's eyes in order for them to be healed? Jesus did it, and the man was healed after he obeyed the command to wash it out in the pool (John 9:6). Some may say, "This goes contrary to good manners and propriety. Why, it is downright offensive! It's inconsistent with God's character." If that is what you think, your thinking is faulty, for God commanded it to be so. *At times, He will offend our minds to test our hearts.*

> "For it is written, 'I will destroy the wisdom of the wise, and will bring to nothing the understanding of the prudent'. (25) Because the foolishness of God is wiser than men, and the weakness of God is stronger than men".
>
> (1 Corinthians 1:19, 25)

Prophetic Words, Signs, Wonders, and Manifestations

While demonic manifestations are unnerving and offensive from the source, God will command prophetic signs and wonders in the last days that *in appearance* could be unnerving or offensive. These manifestations will appear offensive because of a departure from the normal or familiar modes and styles of Christian method and worship.

Always remember that regardless of how normal or "odd" manifestations, signs, etc. may appear, they must ultimately edify the body of Christ and glorify God. Prophetic utterances given through the gift of tongues in a public service without interpretation would be out of order. When interpreted, it brings edification (See 1 Corinthians 12 & 14). Likewise, all prophetic signs and wonders, especially those that depart from what is considered normal, must have interpretation or definition for the sake of the edification of the body of Christ. Anything less is out of order. People will just think you are weird, and they might try to have you locked up! Nothing should ever draw people's attention away from God, but should cause them to want to worship Him more.

Natural Reactions

While all things must be done for edification, one must be careful to allow complete freedom of expression in worship. I have seen people do things in worship that I may never do, but that does not make it wrong. We must not despise or try to control someone's liberty in the Lord. In 2 Samuel 6:15-23, a curse came upon King David's wife, Michal, who despised him when he danced before the Lord in an undignified manner. Let us not judge someone's worship by the way it appears. We could insult the Holy Spirit while trying to maintain and control others with our sense of religious dignity.

We must be careful not to let our natural reactions keep us from perceiving things from God's perspective. It is possible to be so devoted to our concepts of dignity, decency, and order that we miss God. In addition, we must never judge things based on our familiarity with it. The "God has always done it this way, and He is not going to do it any other way" attitude must have no place in us.

Father, divide soul and spirit within us that we may know the difference between those things that originate from sinful flesh and those that come from You, regardless of whether it appears to be good or bad. All praise to Your most awesome and excellent name. Amen.

CHAPTER NINE

Familiarity and Unbelief

Would you recognize Jesus if He revealed Himself to you in a manner with which you were not familiar?

After Jesus was raised from the dead, He appeared to two disciples on the road to Emmaus. They did not recognize Him until He broke bread with them and opened their spiritual eyes. They said:

> "Did not our heart burn within us as He talked with us on the road, and while he opened the Scriptures to us?"
> (Luke 24:32)

Their spiritual discernment was restored in the place of intimate fellowship with the Lord. While they were intently listening to Him, they recognized Him. There was evidence in their hearts of who He was before this time, but they did not recognize it as such. He had died on the cross, and they did not believe they would see Him alive again. Their unbelief took precedence over the witness of the Spirit within them.

The two men on the road to Emmaus considered Christ, according to their fleshly thinking, to be dead, but after He opened their spiritual eyes by removing their unbelief, they were then able to recognize the inner witness of the Spirit. The burning in their hearts signaled this. This burning was something they had probably experienced in being around Him before He died. Yet, it was an indelible mark they could not identify because of their preoccupation with His death. *Jesus' death had become far more familiar or real to them than His life.* Beloved, what are those things that your mind and heart are preoccupied with that would keep you in unbelief and keep you from hearing or discerning God?

The "If Onlys" and "P.M.S."

The disciples were probably saying things like, "If only Jesus had not died, things would be going fine." The "Poor Me Syndrome" (P.M.S.) held them captive. How many of us are so bound up by being preoccupied with what could have been or what we think should be that we cannot enjoy today and be content with the "God Who is Now?" Are we unable to discern the One who is sufficient for us now in spite of all of our "if onlys?"

The two thieves that hung next to Christ on the cross both reviled Him (Matthew 27:44). However, something happened in the heart of one of them (Luke 23:39-43). Perhaps, after hearing Jesus forgive those who had Him crucified, the thief's heart melted. Whatever the case, one thief chose to accept responsibility for his actions, told the other thief that both of them were receiving justice for their deeds, and said that Jesus had done nothing wrong. He obviously sensed his wickedness as contrasted to Christ's goodness and was convicted in his heart. The other thief chose to wallow in self-pity and Jesus did not even acknowledge him. He may have been abused and forsaken by his earthly father and raised by a dysfunctional mother. Nevertheless, he was still accountable to God for the state of his heart. This other thief even asked Jesus to deliver all three of them but was not willing to admit that he deserved exactly what he got. It is possible to call on the Lord and Him not acknowledge us, because He refuses to fit into the package of our expectations. All things must be done on His terms. He requires faith from a childlike heart.

This world is like the ocean liner, the *Titanic*, which sank in 1912 A.D. after hitting an iceberg in the icy waters of the North Atlantic.

It is sinking into the abyss, never to arise again in its corrupted, arrogant state. It was reported that someone said concerning the *Titanic*: "Even God couldn't sink this ship." Even so, the world continues as if it is invincible. All people are sinking into the abyss with the world, but God has provided a Lifeboat for whosoever will come aboard. The Lifeboat is His Son – Jesus Christ. Until we acknowledge our need for Him and that we deserve to sink with "the ship," we will sink into the abyss with it. All people who have not found safety in Christ as their Lifeboat will be subject to the same atrocities as any other person on "the ship." Drowning people are unmerciful, because they will do anything to keep from drowning, even though it is inevitable. No one on the sinking ship is immune to death and to the suffering inflicted by other unmerciful, drowning people. All of us deserve to suffer and "drown" in the abyss according to God's justice, yet, many people are drowning because they refuse to rise above the "if onlys."

If only:

... the ship had not hit the iceberg.
... that person had not gotten on the lifeboat before me.
... the lifeboat would come and save me, I would not be in this mess.
... that insensitive person had not stolen my life vest.
... someone would recognize that I do not deserve to drown.
... people would understand that I had nothing to do with sinking the ship.

"Therefore, just as through one man [Adam] sin entered the world, and death through sin, and thus death spread to all men, because all sinned".
(Romans 5:12)

If only you would admit that you are reaping what you have sown and cry out to the Lord, then He would deliver you. "For let not that man [the one who doubts] suppose that he will receive anything from the Lord" (James 1:7). Does that sound cruel? Do you prefer human sympathy over the truth? "And you shall know

Guidelines for Spiritual Discernment

the truth, and the truth shall make you free" (John 8:32). Do you feel like the other thief who the Lord did not acknowledge? Then cease blaming God and others and stop trying to ease your conscience with the "God allowed it" attitude. Seek to justify God in all of your "if onlys" and He will justify you. May the Lord deliver us from evil hearts of unbelief—hearts that cannot comprehend, recognize, or discern God because of its selfish preoccupation. Even though we cannot be completely blamed for all the bad hands that life has dealt us, we are still accountable to God for the state of our heart toward Him and others. The state of our heart is what justifies or condemns us.

If only:

- ... I was not overweight.
- ... I did not have this big zit on my face.
- ... I had a date with that Bathsheba fox.
- ... I looked like Sharon Stoneheart or Arnold Shortsarebigger.
- ... I was married, then all my problems would be solved.
- ... I was not married to a jerk, then all my problems would be solved.
- ... my mother had not called me stupid.
- ... my daddy had not called me ugly.
- ... that person had not abused me.
- ... white people had not mistreated my ancestors.
- ... I had a ministry like Billy Haygram or Barney Hunn.
- ... these people who the Lord has given me would listen to me.
- ... my church was bigger.
- ... my books and music would sell.
- ... things were like they used to be.
- ... I had not committed that sin.

If only you would turn your heart to the Lord then the blinders would be removed. You would see that your problem does not lie within the "if onlys" of your past but is attributed to the unbelief that is presently in your heart. You would know Him who transcends the past, present, and future, and He would satisfy you with the rivers of His pleasures. In His presence, you would know fullness—filled with joy inexpressible even if the zit remains on your face. Jesus is the answer to all of our "if onlys," and we can only know Him by the Spirit. He will not reveal Himself in the confines of our P.M.S. He seeks to draw us out of it. If only you would accept full responsibility for the state of your heart toward God and stop blaming others, you would see the glory of God as did one of the thieves on the cross.

Knowing Others According to the Spirit

> "Therefore, from now on, we regard no man according to the flesh. Even though we have known Christ according to the flesh, yet now we know Him thus no longer".
> (2 Corinthians 5:16)

The word "regard" is defined as: "to care or have concern for." To "regard someone according to the flesh" would therefore mean: "to care or have concern for another person on the emotional, intellectual, personality level, and independent of the Lord." We cannot know the Lord on this level. On this level, our perception of others would be based on how we outwardly perceive them and on what we expect from them. On this level, we know (discern, perceive, distinguish) and show concern according to our perception of another person's plight, and such fleshly concern is always mixed with self-centeredness. Our care or concern for others must only be according to the mind of the Spirit, and this involves understanding that God is more concerned for people than we are.

For example, Peter regarded the Lord according to the flesh. He sought to prevent Jesus from going to Jerusalem and dying, but He rebuked him sharply (Matthew 16:21-23). (Peter possibly believed and expected the Lord to live and become King of Israel at that time.) He seemed to be sincerely concerned for the Lord, yet that concern was used by the devil to attempt to thwart the purpose of God. His concern for Jesus was rooted in his perception of the pending crisis that would be produced in his life if Jesus died. In other words, Peter had a self-centered concern rooted in

Guidelines for Spiritual Discernment

ignorance and unbelief.

We must be careful not to let our concern or regard for people keep us from rightly perceiving what God is doing in their lives, and thus become a hindrance to them. Our fleshly concerns can blind us to the whole picture. Such could be used by the devil to project on others something other than the will of God and bring confusion into their lives. This type of concern or regard has its roots in the human emotional level but not in the love of Christ. To further explain, we can be in emotional turmoil concerning other people we regard and entirely miss God's heart toward them. Any self-centered emotional bonds that we have toward people that we regard will be the means by which the devil will use us to wrongly influence them. Let us make sure that our thinking is in harmony with the Lord's while showing our concern in relationships (Matthew 16:23). When our concern for others is according to the Spirit, they will be encouraged toward their destiny in Christ.

There are certain people that I enjoy being around because my personality and sense of humor is similar to theirs. (Of course, that does not mean that I do not enjoy being around other people who are different). Yet, I had much rather make a holy connection with them—spirit to spirit. There are some Christians that I have found it hard to connect with spirit to spirit because they live mostly in the mental, emotional, and personality realm.

Our relationship with others must go deeper than the mental, emotional, etc. levels. It must be on the same level in which we can only relate to God, spirit-to-spirit. That which is communicated on the spirit-to-spirit level can then be expressed through the mind, emotions, and personality. We relate to God as a true worshiper, and this is how we must regard one another. If a person is not a true worshiper of God, then they cannot be regarded, on the level that God commands, by those who are. There can be no true Christian fellowship with them. Our initial relationship with them can only be based on our getting them reconciled to God. While all men are called to be true worshipers of God, not everyone worships Him.

Familiarity and Unbelief

Regarding Spiritual Leaders

There are those within the Church who are true believers, but, for various reasons, have tendencies to wrongly look to spiritual leaders for emotional stability. Some become enamored with the personalities, knowledge, and anointing of certain preachers. *There is a point at which our regard for others becomes idolatrous. This happens often on the emotional, intellectual, and personality levels.* We have to be able to distinguish between the person and the Lord in the person or we *will* be deceived.

There have been times in the Church where spiritual leaders have made people dependent upon them and not upon Christ. Such leaders are usually wounded, fearful, insecure, or immature and make wounded and spiritually naive or weak people dependent on them. They take the place of the Holy Spirit in their "followers'" lives. This is an affront to God.

Regarding Family Members

Within the institution of the family, how often have we heard of a son or daughter who, because of having become a Christian, endured hardship at home due to the tendencies of the rest of the family to regard them according to the way they used to be? The family continued to relate to them in a manner with which they were familiar. This is why Jesus said:

> "If anyone comes to Me, and does not hate his father and mother, wife and children, brothers and sisters, yes, and his own life also, he cannot be My disciple".
>
> (Luke 14:26)

After having become a true worshiper of God, one cannot continue to relate to others on fleshly levels even if they are of our immediate family. Such relationships contain the seeds of idolatry. I am referring to a form of idolatry that makes one more dependent on or devoted to a human being than God. What fellowship does light have with darkness? Parents, you need to be careful not to control your teenage children because of emotional bonds you have with them. Do you *need* them to be dependent on you? Is your self-worth wrapped up in that? You must relate to them as mutual worshipers of God (or at least as having the potential of being so). You must see them from God's perspective. Turn them loose so that they can be entirely dependent on God. Is your concern for them and your counsel to them rooted in fears and insecurities that still exist in your life? Are you counseling them according to the mind of the Lord or what you think is wisdom?

Jesus words in response to his mother and brothers' need to speak with Him seemed harsh. He told the crowd, "Who is My mother and who are My brothers?" 'And He stretched out His hand toward His disciples and said,' "Here are My mother and My brothers! (50) For whoever does the will of My Father in heaven is My brother and sister and mother" (Matthew 12: 48-50). Most of us have probably heard the saying, "blood is thicker than water" in reference to our earthly family. However, Jesus showed no partiality to His earthly family as opposed to anyone else who does the will of God. Possibly, His family had certain expectations of Him to be partial in some way or allow them "special" privileges. They may have gone away at that point thinking, "He doesn't really care for us. We are His family and He is not giving us the attention we deserve." They may have also been influenced by some of what the "reputable" religious leaders were saying about Him. Whatever the case, Jesus would not allow Himself to come under the corrupt control of any person—even His immediate family. Yes, He honored His mother and father but only fellowshipped with those who walked in the light.

My relationship with my wife started on a spiritual level. I saw her as a steadfast "house of prayer and worship." It was not her wonderful personality, intelligence, or outward beauty that initially attracted me. (Now, I would have to say that her cooking did play a role in that. She is a full-blooded, Tuscany Italian.) She became a person with whom I loved to pray and worship (and eat with). It is interesting to note that since our marriage in 1991, it has sometimes been difficult for us to pray and worship together due to our outward familiarity with one another.

Familiarity and Unbelief

We all have expectations toward others, especially within the confines of the marriage covenant. Expectations can often be based on outward *appearance* and are for the most part selfish. If our expectations are not met, then we are prone to make fleshly judgments or assessments against our mate. This, however, will hinder our ability to pray and worship together on a one on one basis. Therefore, *our expectations toward people cannot take precedence over our fulfilling our responsibilities toward them.* This mainly involves our responsibility to pray for them. As we pray for people, we will begin to see them through Heaven's eyes. We will become hateful if we let our lives center on our personal expectations. There is nothing wrong with having expectations toward others; however, we must make sure that our self-worth or loving others does not depend on the fulfillment of them.

If we are prone to have our feelings hurt, then we need to make some adjustments in the way we perceive and relate to others. Hurt feelings are indicative of a hidden, selfish motivation. We are "unprofitable servants" (Luke 17:5-10) and should not even expect a "thank you" from the Master or anyone else. Of course, this does not mean we will not receive "thank yous." The problem lies in the expectation of it. If we will maintain this attitude in our relationship with other people, understanding that any service done for them is first to be done as unto the Lord, then we will be free to love and serve as Jesus would. Those who have pure hearts in their service to the Lord will diffuse the aroma of His pleasure and favor.

The main character in the movie *"Chariots of Fire,"* Eric Liddel, left the mission field in China to represent Scotland as a runner in the Olympics. He became England's greatest hope for a gold medal. In the movie, his explanation to his sister for leaving the mission field for a time was something like: "When I run, I sense His [God's] pleasure." We are to run *this race* for God's pleasure alone in spite of what other people do or do not do. "For of Him and through Him and to Him are all things, to whom be glory forever. Amen" (Romans 11:36). Can we be content in this life with just having our Father's pleasure and no one else's? Our self-worth cannot live or die by what we attempt to get from serving others. We only have

God's pleasure because of our faith walk (Hebrews 11:6), and faith excludes boasting in ourselves, our works or successes, and in others (Romans 3:27).

Do we have more faith in God's ability to work in people or in our ability to demand the fulfillment of our expectations? Does our ability to demand something from someone have power to change them? Can or should someone do something just because we demand or expect it? Does God give us the right to be angry and offended with or judge someone else because they have not lived up to our expectations? Could it be that our expectations are selfish, unrealistic, or are pointed in the wrong direction? All of our expectations toward others should first be mixed with humility, meekness, and faith, and then presented to the Lord in prayer. Failure to do this will *always* cause offense. Let us make sure that we are not reacting with our natural eyes to what we see or expect to see. Whatever is not born out of faith toward God is sin (Romans 14:23).

For example, look at this hypothetical situation. Let us say that I have a close friend who I never would expect to drink alcoholic beverages. One day, I go over to his house, and after being invited in to his living, I find that he is drinking a beer. He is not drunk and does not intend to be, but I do not take that into consideration. More than likely, I will become offended and disappointed because I am "too good" to drink beer and, therefore, those I regard should be also. Before talking to him about it, I wrongly judge him. I am convinced (but he is not) that drinking all alcoholic beverages is wrong, so I attempt to persuade him otherwise, but he does not agree, resulting in me labeling him a compromiser. In my self-righteousness, I have judged him solely on what I saw outwardly. Out of what would seem to be sincere concern, I have attempted to impose my conviction on him, yet failed to know what the mind of the Lord is in the matter. Could it be that my friend has the freedom to drink beer even though I may not?

Even if my friend was committing a sin, am I putting more faith in my ability to point out what is wrong, thinking that will change him, or in God's ability to convict and change him. Can you counter sin with another sin? *In whatever way we do not have faith in God for another person we will only know them after the flesh.* Faith in

God is the foundation for healthy relationships with others. Otherwise, we will be trying to get from people what we should be getting from God. Our failing to pray for other people proves our lack of faith in God for them. Instead, they become people who we wrongly expect and demand things from.

Of course, in the above scenario, I am not talking about having liberty to sin. Christ's Lordship gives us no such liberty. It is idolatrous to try to draw life from anything besides the Lord. He is our refuge and not alcoholic beverages. We can only truly enjoy this life by first finding our security, contentment, and comfort in the Lord.

We are not to regard anyone according to the flesh because it is self-centered and contradicts God's love. The consequent end is that we become bound up in unbelief and are left to our own understanding. We must take the necessary steps to secure our being able to flow in the Spirit with those we regard by drawing out their true spirituality as worshipers of God and not relating to and judging them as people who are supposed to meet our expectations. *If we are free to worship God and pray together with our mate or the person we regard, then we will have no unmet expectations.* Let us make sure that our relationship with others is not based on an outward and self-centered familiarity with them.

Regarding Church Services

Much of our familiarity with the Lord centers on Sunday morning Church services. We have mistakenly given the names "church" and "Christianity" to our preoccupation with self-imposed religious deadness. We sing a few worship songs, make announcements, receive the offering, preach a sermon, and possibly experience various anointings (not necessarily in that order). Afterward, we go home with more knowledge *about* God and a possible spiritual "high" only to return next week in much the same spiritual state that we were in the preceding week. We continue in this state as if that is all there is to God and wonder why we cannot have lasting impact on society. It is insane for us to think that we can do the same things repeatedly and still expect different results. Oh, if we would only live in the shadow of the judgment seat of Christ.

To what degree has the glory of man's flesh (his personality, emotions, intelligence, and charisma) become the mesmerizing influence within the Church? Have we in our spiritual slumber allowed the withering glory of flesh to weave its web of deceit while Jesus is left outside knocking? Men can be anointed by God and still draw our hearts away from Him. Anointing does not validate the vessel before God. Balaam gave one of the most powerful prophecies over Israel in the Bible, but God had the Israelites kill him because of his wickedness that was spawned by greed (Numbers 22-25; 31:8). This is proof that we need more than just the anointing. We need the Anointed One. He promised:

> "I will dwell in them and walk among them. I will be their God, and they shall be My people".
> (2 Corinthians 6:16b)

In John 14:21, Jesus also promised that He and His Father would love those who keep His commandments and that He (Jesus) would reveal Himself to them.

May our worship of God go beyond familiarity with Him as revealed through others. Some of that familiarity can be based on misconceptions that originate from men and not from God.

> Jesus admonished the Jews in Mark 7:6,
> "... Well did Isaiah prophesy of you hypocrites, as it is written: 'this people honors Me with their lips, but their heart is far from Me. (7) And in vain do they worship Me, teaching as doctrines the commandments of men.' (8) For laying aside the commandment of God, you hold the tradition of men...."

From this passage one could define the "traditions of men" as any religious observance, form, or agenda adhered to as godly service or worship that is an attempt on our part to try to get God to bless, set his approval on, or be a part of what we are doing.

Familiarity and Unbelief

It involves putting more faith in our service or observance rather than in God. We gain God's favor or approval only through the blood of Christ. Therefore, true worship and service always attracts God's presence because it focuses on what Jesus has done for us and is presently doing and not on what we do. Anything less is vain. God requires a broken heart and a contrite spirit (Psalm 51:16, 17). He never refuses such offerings. When we come before Him in this manner, we will be accepted. If we do not, we will be rejected like Cain (Genesis 4:1-8), and will attract the honor of men but not the honor of God. The Lord accepts nothing that originates from us.

What if God's presence came and interrupted our Sunday morning comfort zones? What if His presence moved in upon us and became the central focus of the meeting, replacing the rigid programs and agendas of men with which we have become so familiar? We would be changed or we would have to leave. Remember that all the Old Testament sacrifices, rituals, cleansings, and symbolism pointed to the One whose presence filled the Holy of Holies. Apart from that Presence, all the sacrifices, rituals, etc. were empty. All service performed by the priests in the temple would have been dead works. What does God think about the sacrifices and services you offer to Him?

What if God visited us in such a manner that upset our understanding of church, ministry, and the Christian walk? What if He revealed to us that our works are wood, hay, and stumble and will not withstand the fire of His judgment? It is time to ask the Lord if we are trying to get Him to bless what we are doing instead of getting into what *He* is doing. The reason we are not experiencing and maintaining His fire and glory in our meetings is that our sacrifices are not acceptable to Him. We must stop offering to Him the old, familiar, and comfortable wineskins of rigidly structured meetings. *It is time for spiritual leaders to take their place as facilitators, coaches, or overseers instead of being territorial, insecure lords.* Our hearts can be so insensitive and our wills set so much on our agendas that we do not discern that God is displeased. Even so, there are times when He blesses with His presence in spite of us and not because He is pleased. This is because of His great mercy (He loves us) and not because of our obedience.

The Lord desires to reveal Himself to us as He did to the two on the road to Emmaus. He did not reveal Himself to them because of their faith. It was so that they would be free from their unbelief. Their unbelief was rooted in their knowledge of His death and their ignorance of His resurrection life. The Lord desires to rekindle the flame in our heart that was brought to smoldering embers because of our regarding and trying to know Him and others according to the flesh and not seeing with the eyes of the Spirit. He will not condemn us for the consequent unbelief, but will lovingly rebuke us as He opens our eyes. Will you allow Him to do that for you? He is risen and has ascended on High.

Father, may we come to know Jesus in ways with which we are not familiar and comfortable, and may You give us eyes to recognize Him and a heart to receive Him when He appears. May we also recognize the many ways in which we have regarded others according to the flesh, and have put more faith in our ability to complain and demand the fulfillment of our expectations than in You.

Lord, we desire to be perfect worshipers of You. Amen.

CHAPTER TEN

Personal Likes, Dislikes, Fears, and Insecurities

All spiritual leaders should stay prepared, studying to show themselves approved by God, in order to effectively proclaim the word of God to the people. However, whether or not a minister *likes to* use notes when presenting a message does not determine spirituality or effectiveness. The degree of God's life as opposed to the self-life flowing through the minister will determine that. Preparation time and notes may assist some ministers in revealing Jesus to the people more effectively; however, such should never be used just so that he or she can preach a good sermon. Some people like spontaneity, and some like structure. In any case, one must be more devoted to what God desires instead of what *we like*.

We do not have a problem with a minister preparing a sermon or using notes, correct? If we do not, then we probably would not have a problem with a worship team practicing before a service. Then what about choreographed dancing in a church service as a worship presentation? The problem some would have with such centers on that word "choreographed." (My desire here is not to defend choreographed dancing or anything else, but to promote true discernment. I am using this as an example from my own experience.)

According to the *Microsoft Bookshelf 98* dictionary, the term *choreograph* is defined: *"To plan out or oversee the movement, development, or details of; orchestrate."* That sounds a lot like what some ministers would do with a sermon before preaching it, or what a worship team would do with the songs and music before worship service. Better yet, the Lord obviously did this before He created the heavens and the earth. The Spirit of the Lord hovered over that which needed God's choreographic design (His order) at the beginning of creation.

> "And the earth was without form and void, and darkness was upon the face of the deep. And the Spirit of God moved upon the face of the waters".
>
> (Genesis 1:2)

God is the author of creative choreography, and His Spirit is waiting to move upon the design that is born out of communion with Him. To condemn something based on whether or not it is choreographed is not justified by Scripture. We must ask in any case: "Does it point us to the Lord or is it a 'show?' Is it born of His Spirit or the designs of people?" This goes back to knowing the spirit and motivation of those who are involved. We cannot base our judgments in such matters on personal whims, preferences, and dislikes. We may not like the way something *appears* or sounds to us but that does not make it wrong. There are certain styles and methods that I am not drawn to that other Christians may use, but I cannot pass judgment based on that.

Will God use something that has already been planned out by men? He will as long as He originated the design and is given freedom to express Himself through it. I have been used to give prophecies spontaneously and other times the Lord has given me things weeks ahead of time. One is no more anointed than the other. Some people like the spontaneous and others like more structure. God uses both. Understand that God plans even the spontaneous flow of the Spirit. So, this is not an issue of pitting spontaneity against structure or preplanning. We must rightly discern the originator of both. If it is of God, it will point people to Him.

Fears and Insecurities

Another example from my experience is that some leaders place restrictions on the people in reference to the use of the gift of prophecy and other gifts of the Spirit in the church service. There are various reasons for such restrictions, ranging from it being for the sake of order to it being a thing of tradition. In some cases, an individual or a few people may have gotten out of order, so a decision was made to place restrictions on all of the people. While such restrictions are not normally intended to intimidate or to be controlling, nevertheless, they still are. If you are a spiritual leader, please seek God often for wisdom in making righteous judgments in such matters. We must refrain from placing restraints on the sheep that frustrate the God-given liberty they should have in worship.

Decisions made by spiritual leaders must not be based on personal likes or dislikes, and neither on choosing the path of least resistance. It is much easier just to completely do away with something or restrict it than to deal with the problems that may arise through it because of the flesh or immature sheep. All spiritual leaders must be secure in this truth: *your spiritual authority to discern and correct error exceeds the power of error itself.* Being completely secure in this promotes a healthy atmosphere in which the sheep can grow.

For the sake of "order" and to safeguard the sheep, how many "fences" have been built by leaders in the Church that mainly serve their insecurities and fears? If we are self-serving in our leadership role then our judgments in reference to the sheep will also be self-serving. We will not be able to see much beyond what our physical eyes and ears see and hear because of our impure heart. Because of fear and insecurity, we will focus mostly on what is wrong instead of what is right. Furthermore, the way we perceive and relate to those we are responsible to and for will determine our true success as a leader. So, are we going to put more faith in the flesh and its potential to err than in God and His ability to bring us to perfect, liberating order? If a spiritual leader's discernment is truly Spirit-led, God's order will be established.

What if, while a minister is teaching or preaching, someone

begins to make certain noises, and it distracts people from listening to the message? Would it be safe to assume that all such noises is of the flesh or demonic? There have been times in meetings where I have had spiritual travail come upon me, even though it was not coming upon other people. At other times, spiritual travail came upon many people while someone was ministering the word of God. There have also been times where people have cried out under conviction and some were caught up with inexpressible joy while certain ministers were preaching. Obviously, the Spirit of God was confirming His word with signs and wonders. It so happens that He chose to do so before the minister finished his sermon. (Maybe the ministers preaching needed to be interrupted.) A spiritual leader must be careful not to attribute what may be of God as being of the flesh just because his or her sermon is interrupted.

On the other hand, if I am in a meeting and spiritual travail comes on me and not on any one else, then I will leave the meeting and go to a place where I will not disturb others, or I will, if possible, quietly intercede where I am. If what I am experiencing is not in the general flow of what the Spirit of God is corporately doing in a meeting, then I am obligated not to disturb others and trust that, if it is God's will, that He will reveal to the leadership that others need to experience what I am experiencing.

Father, help us not to center our lives and church services on our personal likes and dislikes. Help us to know also how to be more dependent on You in making any decision in relation to your Church. If we are allowing our fear and insecurities to influence our decisions, reveal it to us, forgive us, and set us free, in Jesus' name. Amen.

CHAPTER ELEVEN

Self-righteousness

Jesus declared to the Jews of His day, "Judge not according to the appearance, but judge righteous judgment" (John 7:24). In this context, the Jews were condemning Him for healing a man on the Sabbath. He told them (vs. 22, 23):

"Moses therefore gave you circumcision (not that it is from Moses, but from the fathers), and you circumcise a man on the Sabbath. (23) If a man receives circumcision on the Sabbath, so that the Law of Moses should not be broken, are you angry with Me because I made a man completely well on the Sabbath?"

They had given their whole heart to a self-imposed standard and, consequently, did not have the capacity for love and mercy. *They valued procedure more than people.* Self-righteousness always focuses on outward conformity and appearance, and the resulting judgments are based on what one sees with the eyes and hears with the ears. It is created by the sweat of human effort and ingenuity disguised as religious service rather than by the inward work of God through the Holy Spirit.

We cannot judge righteously as long as we are peering down on others like a vulture from our pinnacle of self-righteousness. It is self-righteous to judge another and have no love in your heart for that person. This judging involves labeling someone but not having a heart for them. It is demanding conformity to a standard of right and wrong but failing to see that God's love is the standard. God does not even give us the right to make good or bad assessments about someone with no godly love in our hearts for them. Apart from God's love, even our perception of good is tainted.

At one time, I complained to my wife that she was not listening to and valuing what I was saying. The Lord rebuked me for doing this because He said that I was doing the same thing to Him that I said my wife had been doing to me. Was I not being self-righteous?

Self-righteousness always finds fault with others but provides a pseudo-covering for our own faults and keeps us from seeing them. If we desire to be listened to and have what we say valued by others, then we need to be good listeners in our relationship with others. We must value what others have to say—especially the Lord. We reap what we sow. If we will deal with the darkness in us first, then, and only then, can we correctly deal with it in others.

Remember, people of God, you cannot demand outward conformity to your knowledge of right and wrong. As a church leader, you may get some to conform to such standards *because of their loyalty to you*, but not because of their loyalty to Christ. So, do you want to compete with Christ for the affections and loyalty of His people? I think not.

Do we condemn others in order to justify ourselves? On the other hand, do we flatter (praise) others for selfish gain?

> "Let me not, I pray you, accept any man's person, neither let me give flattering titles unto man. (22) For I know not to give flattering titles; in so doing my maker would soon take me away".
>
> (Job 32:21-22; KJV)

Those who are not secure in the righteousness that is of faith (Romans 3:27—the righteousness that excludes boasting in others and ourselves) will seek the fallen Adamic way to establish their own and to console, affirm, and fulfill themselves and others by fleshly means. The standard of righteousness thus achieved will come short of God's glory each time.

Self-righteousness

"For I say to you, that unless your righteousness exceeds the righteousness of the scribes and Pharisees, you will by no means enter into the kingdom of heaven".

(Matthew 5:20)

"How can you believe, who receive honor [flattery] from one another, and do not seek the honor that comes from the only God"?

(John 5:44)

The only means to true righteousness does not come from the praise of men. It comes from faith in Christ Jesus our Lord.

"But to him who does not work [those who put no trust in anything originating from themselves or others] but believes in Him who justifies the ungodly, his faith is accounted for righteousness".

(Romans 4:5)

There have been times when I have heard people ask a relative of a person who had died if they had been "saved" preceding death. On occasion, the response would be similar to, "Yes, I remember when he was a boy that he went to the altar and gave his heart to Jesus." Yet, one must ask: if he truly was saved or born again why did he die an alcoholic who was abusive toward his wife and children? Where was the evidence of His faith in God? Someone might respond: "Well, God is the judge but we are not. He knows his heart?" But, what about where Christ said that we would know them by their fruits. He exhorts us to inspect the fruit of people's lives to know whether they are true believers—to know whether their righteousness is of God. Hebrews 12:8 proclaims, "But if you are without chastening, of which all have become partakers, then you are illegitimate and not sons." True sons of God have the evidence of His correction in their lives. If a person does not have this evidence, God is not their Father. God's correction brings about transformation in our lives, and we will yield to it, if we truly have faith in Him. (I say these things understanding that some people do experience what has been called "deathbed" or "foxhole" conversions to Christ.)

A one-time experience does not determine whether someone is justified before God in this life. (Of course, when we first responded with a repentant heart to the Gospel, we were justified or born again—we were given a new spirit.) The Apostle Paul made it clear in Romans 4, when he wrote about how Abraham was justified before God, that all people (not just Jews) can be justified if they "...walk in the *steps* of the faith which our father Abraham had while still uncircumcised" (v.12; italics mine). We are justified before God by walking in faith in Jesus Christ everyday. "For we have become partakers of Christ if we hold the beginning of our confidence *steadfast to the end*" (Hebrews 3:14; italics mine). We must follow in the steps or footprints of Abraham's faith or we are not justified but condemned before God. In other words, the Lord requires a lifestyle of faith and repentance toward Him and not just a one-time "fire insurance" deal.

It is not what a person claims with His mouth that justifies him or her, but it is the proof of their faith in God by their walk. People can have a reputation of being good and righteous, have an appearance of godliness, and even claim to be saved but still not be righteous before God. They could be void of true faith in Him. "But do you want to know, O foolish man, that faith without works is dead? (21) Was not Abraham our father justified by works when he offered Isaac his son on the altar... (24) You see then that a man is justified by works, and not by faith only" (James 2:20, 21)? Faith is proven by its works (obedience) and is motivated by compassion and love, otherwise, it is not faith. Abraham had already proven his faith in God by obeying His command to leave his relatives and go into another country, however, he was declared to be "justified" because of the proof of his faith in God many years later. This proves that justification involves not just a one-time expression of faith in God but a continuation in it. We are saved through faith and that salvation is secure as long as we continue in faith. Anything less than this type of righteousness is self-made and demonic.

"Examine yourselves as to whether you are in the faith. Test yourselves. Do you not know yourselves, that Jesus

Self-righteousness

Christ is in you? ——unless indeed you are disqualified".
(2 Corinthians 13:5)

True faith in God will never wrongly find fault with another person, but is fully assured of the ability of God's grace to transform them. Anything less is self-righteous.

Father, help us to know the difference between self-righteousness and Your righteousness and how it applies in all the practicalities of daily life. Help us to know when we are seeing others through eyes of self-righteousness instead of Yours. Purify our hearts to seek Your honor and no other. Thank you, in Jesus' excellent name. Amen.

CHAPTER TWELVE

Some Other Important Issues

In concluding this section, consider the miracle of Jesus turning water into wine (John 2:1-11). This did not really help anyone as far as getting them delivered, healed, or set free from sin. It would seem that all it did was provide them wine during a wedding because they had run out. If a person judged this only by what this miracle did for those people attending the wedding, they might condemn it as not being of God. However, we know that this cannot be the case because the Lord did it. The key here is in verse 11:

"This beginning of miracles Jesus did in Cana of Galilee, and manifested His glory; and His disciples believed in Him."

If God desires to reveal His glory, He will do so whether it fits into our thinking or not. In this case, His ultimate purpose was to increase the faith of His disciples. God is doing things like that today and for no other purpose.

A couple that we know who pastor a church was at their table eating spaghetti and suddenly the wife began to sense a metal taste in her mouth. After looking in the mirror, she found that a tooth, which had partially broken off at an earlier date, was in some measure filled with gold. Later, the tooth was completely filled in. As the result, other people in the church began to get gold fillings. While there are no similar signs recorded in Scripture, God was manifesting His glory and building the faith of His people. The people's faith was encouraged because of this. Not only that, it saved some from having to go to a dentist.

What if it had not produced the intended results? Does that mean it is not of God? Even after Jesus performed many signs, wonders, and miracles before the eyes of His disciples, they still had a problem with unbelief (Matthew 8:26; 16:8). Could that happen today? It *is* happening.

Well, someone might say, "You're not supposed to follow after signs, wonders, etc." That is true, but it does not make these things fleshly or demonic if people do. People followed Jesus for what He could give them and not because they believed. He offended them with the truth, and they stopped following Him (John 6). *Do not confuse the true things of God with what people's wrong motives seem to make of them. True discernment involves being able to separate the two.*

Truths in Review

1. Since witches speak in a demonic counterfeit of the gift of tongues, then God's people should not speak in tongues at all. Is this an example of true discernment? Why or why not?
2. Name some other things besides the gifts of tongues to which this would apply. Think of similarities between Christianity and other religions.
3. Have you read any books or heard any teaching that take this approach to prove movements or certain signs, wonders, and manifestations to be erroneous? If so, how do you feel about such a book now?
4. What are some things that we can learn from the Prophet Samuel to help develop our ability to hear God?
5. If it is not in the Bible then it cannot be of God. Is this statement applicable in every situation? Why or why not?
6. If a manifestation, sign, or wonder takes place and there is nothing in the Bible similar to it, how can we know whether it is of God?

Some Other Important Issues

7. How can our natural reactions hinder our discernment? Think of some scenarios where your natural reactions could hinder your discernment.
8. Suppose you saw someone do something during a worship service that you have never done or seen before. It makes you uncomfortable. Could it be that the discomfort you are feeling is the Holy Spirit telling you that something is wrong or are you uncomfortable because the person's freedom is a threat to your bondage? How would you know the difference?
9. In the corporate Church meeting, I can do whatever I have an urge to do in spite of what anybody thinks. True or false? Why or why not?
10. What would prevent us from rejecting Christ if He revealed Himself to us in a way with which we are not familiar—in a way that exceeds and seemingly contradicts our experience and beliefs?
11. What is the difference between knowing or regarding someone according to the flesh and according to the Spirit?
12. How does unbelief affect our ability to "see" God?
13. If I do not like the way something is done in a church meeting, does that make it wrong? Name some ways in which your personal likes and comfort zones could cause you to wrongly judge others.
14. What is the one thing that spiritual leaders must have full assurance of in order to provide the best atmosphere in which the people they oversee can grow?
15. How does self-righteousness affect our discernment? Can you think of times in your life where you were self-righteously critical of others?
16. Spiritual leaders are our most affective weapons against deception. True or false? Why or why not?.

Part Four

Correct Biblical Interpretation

"Be diligent to present yourself approved of God, a worker who does not need to be ashamed, rightly dividing the word of truth".

(2 Timothy 2:15)

During my life as a Christian, I have encountered differing interpretations of Scripture. There have been times when I had to confront error, some of which challenged me to dig deeper into God's heart and His written word for answers. This was attributed to my not being secure in some of what I believed. My defensive reactions were the evidences that proved this was so. There is a difference between head knowledge and knowing something in your heart.

One thing that has become clear to me is that it really matters what you believe concerning doctrine or the truth of God's word. *What you believe will determine how you perceive and relate to God, and this will determine how you perceive and relate to humanity.*

Jesus addressed the Scriptural views of the religious leaders during His days on earth. Their insecurity concerning what they believed was evident in their questioning His authority, and their belief system was the support for their self-righteousness. The chief priests and the elders came to Him while He was teaching and said:

> "By what authority are you doing these things? And who gave You this authority"?
>
> (Matthew 21:23)

They could not spiritually discern that Jesus was the Messiah because they were more devoted to their teachings than to God. What Jesus taught was revealed to Him by the Father, but they only taught what was taught them by men and what they concluded by their understanding. This was true in spite of their great knowledge of Scripture.

> "And it came to pass, when Jesus had ended these sayings, the people were astonished at His doctrine; (29) for He taught them as one having authority, and not as the scribes".
>
> (Matthew 7:28-29)

Those who receive revelation from God will also have the authority to speak for God. Those who merely teach the traditions of men will have no life-giving authority before God. They only speak for men and cannot impart life. Therefore, it is important that what we believe doctrinally or concerning any truth originates from God and not from men. We are to speak or teach, as God's mouthpiece, only those things that come by means of revelation from Him and not what is concluded by our logic or teaching that comes from others. *Logic (the product of our thinking or deductive reasoning) should be formed only out of revelation from God, but true revelation from God is never produced by logic. Apart from being founded on revelation from God, logic is rooted in pride.*

CHAPTER THIRTEEN

In Whom Do You Boast?

"Jesus answered them and said, 'My doctrine is not Mine, but His who sent Me. (17) If anyone wills to do His will, he shall know concerning the doctrine, whether it is from God or whether I speak on My own authority. (18) He who speaks from himself seeks his own glory; but He who seeks the glory of the One who sent Him is true, and no unrighteousness is in Him'".

(John 7:16-18)

What we believe must come by revelation from God or we will only be mouthing words (although perhaps with passion and skill) and have no true authority to instruct others. We will be drawing attention to ourselves and not causing people to discern and experience God. We may even establish a following from spiritually naive or immature people who will quote us as if we are speaking for God. "He who speaks from himself seeks his own glory..." There is nothing wrong with honoring those through whom we believed because of the truth that came (comes) to us through them (1 Corinthians 3:5). This holds true as long as we realize that:

"...Neither he who plants is anything, nor he who waters, but God who gives the increase," and (21) "Therefore, let no one boast in men. For all things are yours: (22)

whether Paul or Apollos or Cephas, or the world or life or death, or things present or things to come – all are yours. (23) And you are Christ's, and Christ is God's".
(1 Corinthians 3:7, 21-23)

We have had many people eat with us in our home, some of whom had small children. A common characteristic of children is that they are very fond of their mother's cooking, and they do not mind letting you know it. They might say things like "Your spaghetti's good, but my mom's is better" or they may not eat your cooking at all. This can be expected from children, even though it may not be appropriate or mannerly, but something similar is going on in the Church.

If all things are ours then why do we exalt certain ministers that we are fond of as if the best of all those things come only through them? Note: I am not saying that truth cannot come *through* men, because even Scripture was given by inspiration from the Holy Spirit through holy men according to 2 Peter 1:20-21.

The point is that any interpretation of Scripture that is a product of mere logic will bear no authority or life from God, yet it can still be very persuasive. It is easy to confuse such persuasiveness with God's authority. Listen to Paul's words on this matter:

> "And I, brethren, when I came to you, did not come with excellence of speech or of wisdom, declaring to you the testimony of God. (2) For I determined not to know any thing among you except Jesus Christ and Him crucified. (3) I was with you in weakness, in fear, and in much trembling. (4) And my speech and my preaching were not with persuasive words of human wisdom, but in demonstration of the Spirit and of power, (5) that your faith should not stand in the wisdom of men but in the power of God".
> (1 Corinthians 2:1-5)

The source of much of the division that exists in the Church today comes from God's people being overly fond of or devoted to a minister or organization. These divisive sects build walls of exclusivism that keep out what they would call error and, unfortunately, keeps God's fullness out. These are "high places" in the hearts of God's people that must be torn down. God is a jealous over His people. Listen to the word of the Lord through the prophet Jeremiah (5:30, 31):

"An astonishing and horrible thing has been committed in the land: (31) the prophets prophesy falsely, and the priests rule by their own power; and My people love to have it so. But what will you do in the end?"

In other words, the spiritual leaders were judging, teaching, and interpreting Scripture from themselves and the people loved it. This statement made by Jesus is appropriate:

> "I have come in my Father's name, and you do not receive me: if another comes in his own name, him you will receive".
>
> (John 5:43)

This boasting in flesh is a form of idolatry. The people were probably saying things like, "Wow, that guy can prophesy!" or "Wasn't that a great sermon! He has a lot of revelation!" or "Boy, she really has a lot of wisdom" or "I only listen to the teaching and preaching of Reverend _____." Yet, what will we do in the end when we have to stand before the judgment seat of Christ and give an account for rejecting Him and honoring withering flesh? What if we find out that we have been more devoted to an ideology[iii] than to Christ? In the end, we will wish that we did not *love to have it so.* The Lord calls it an astonishing and horrible thing. If we are doing something that is horrible to the Lord, it would be far better that we know and repent of it now.

> In 1 Corinthians 3:3-4, Paul sternly rebuked that church:
> "...For you are still carnal. For where there are envy, strife, and divisions among you, are you not carnal and behaving like mere men? For when one says, 'I am of Paul,' and another, 'I am of Apollos', are you not carnal?"

The chief characteristic of being carnal is defined in Romans 8:7. It clearly reveals that a carnal mind is an enemy of or hostile to God. It will not and cannot subject itself to God. A carnal mind signifies an impure and hardened heart that cannot rightly discern, interpret, or distinguish God, and, consequently, *one is only left with the option to be led by or to boast in men.* This was happening in the church at Corinth and it is happening today.

There are those who are so loyal to a minister that such a one could do no wrong or teach no error in their eyes. My Father in Heaven once told me that if you follow any person too closely, you could fall into the same ditch into which they might fall. Our devotion to and fondness of a minister, church, or Christian organization cannot exceed our devotion to the Truth—Christ Jesus our Lord. "...God is light and in Him is no darkness at all" (1 John 1:5). It is enlightening to note that this statement is not made about any human being or organization. There is NO darkness in God. There IS darkness in every human being. We must realize this, no matter how much certain people have done for us, and how much they have meant to us. There is only one true hero and His name is Jesus Christ. There are great men and women in the body of Christ, but this is only because God has made them that way. They are only great because they have become the least—servants. If God's presence lifted from them, they would either become the most successful "Pharisee" or the worst sinner.

Beloved, how do you relate to or regard your pastor or other leaders in the body of Christ? Do they have your loyalty or does Christ? Pastors and spiritual leaders, do you spend more time making the people loyal to you and your church than to Christ? If they are truly loyal and rightly connected to their Head, they will do what He tells them to do and serve where He tells them to serve. Faithfulness will not be a problem.

Notes

iii Webster's New Riverside Dictionary defines "ideology" as *a body of ideas characteristic of a person, group, culture, or political party.*

CHAPTER FOURTEEN

Recognizing Persuasive Words

If you can be deceived by the persuasive words of people in one little area, that can open the door for further compromise, and you will find yourself boasting in and being overly devoted to a minister or organization as opposed to God. A little leaven will leaven the whole lump of bread. Truth mixed with a little persuasive error is dangerous.

While I was at Bible College, there were certain teachers who always caused a quickening in my spirit because of the truth that was coming through them. The Lord used them to help ground me in doctrinal truth. My spirit recognized the truth coming through them and loved it—my spirit would leap within me. God has made us this way.

Our spirits are made to react to truth and error; however, it is possible to be deceived by allowing another spirit to persuade us on the mental or emotional level. Possibly, the most difficult deception to overcome is when a person has been seduced through persuasive words to believe something that is not Biblical truth. Usually, this happens while a teacher or preacher is speaking by true revelation and then subtly throws out "revelation" that is product of their understanding. The devil is so good at his craft that, if we do not remain vigilant, he will seduce us into bypassing the process of true discernment in us through the mesmerizing influence that a man or woman may have over us. A look at some synonyms of the word "mesmerizing" will shed more light on how the enemy deceives us: "gripping, compelling, attention-grabbing, exciting, thrilling, interesting." These words define what Paul meant when he asked the Galatians, "Who has *bewitched* you, that you should not obey the truth" (italics mine). While a speaker may thrill, excite, and intrigue us, we cannot be so "gripped" by them that we fail to discern that they are not teaching the truth. The enemy uses such to sneak error past our spiritual discernment.

During the process of deception, a person is conditioned by the persuasive teacher to come to conclusions concerning the Lord and Scripture through their own understanding, and the "switch" to the inherent witness of the Spirit is unwittingly placed in the "off" position. Afterward, they are subtly taught to violate rules of Biblical interpretation. One incentive to keep us from being deceived in this manner is to always remember that our leaning on our understanding is rooted in pride, and that God resists or opposes the proud. The proud are those who think they see or know the truth but actually do not. The things of the Kingdom of God are hidden *from* them, but are hidden *for* and revealed to the "babes."

The Apostle Paul described this process in terms of what could be referred to as the *principle of courtship and exclusion*. This principle can be used in both a good and an evil way. A good example is when Paul used it to win the Galatians back to the true Gospel (Galatians 4:18). The evil example is revealed in the way the false teachers bewitched the Galatians. "They zealously court you, but for no good; yes, they want to exclude you, that you may be zealous for them" (Galatians 4:17). To clarify what Paul was saying, the word "court" would best be defined: "to desire earnestly." For what purpose does a man court a woman? The obvious answer is so that he will win her affections. His main objective is so that she will have the same affections, admiration, and loyalty to him for the rest of her life, as opposed to anyone else. In a similar way, the false teachers were trying to win the affections, admiration, and loyalty of the Galatian church as revealed in the last part of the above verse: "...that you may be zealous for them." The word "zealous" here is the same Greek word translated previously as "zealously court."

Now that we understand the process, what method did the false teachers use to bewitch the Galatians? The key to the answer is found in the word "exclude." It conveys the idea of being turned away at the door of someone's home or of not being allowed entrance. The false teachers were persuasively making the truth of the Gospel look bad and were making their error look good to the Galatians. (Does this remind you of what the serpent did to Eve in the Garden of Eden?) This involved convincing them that they were not justified before God unless they adhered to the false teachings. As the result, this made the Galatians feel like they were excluded from what was promoted as being the "best and highest way." By their undying commitment (zeal), the false teachers accomplished their objective. They used their words like a hammer, through the fear and praise of men, to mold the Galatians into their self-imposed and self-made religious image (Galatians 1:10-12). One could conclude from all of this that any person who ongoingly tolerates error will eventually believe it. The Galatians should have never tolerated it from the beginning.

Now, we will look at other examples of how this persuasiveness works.

God and Man Distinguished

After God created Adam's body from the dust of the earth, He breathed into him the breath of life. God took a part of Himself and put it into Adam at that point and He became a living soul (1 Corinthians 15:45). That part of Himself that God breathed into man became his spirit. Whoaaaaaaa! How many of you were going along with what I just said? What is wrong with it? First, Genesis 6:17 and 7:15, 22 all indicate that animals also have the breath of life in them. Secondly, if God imparted a part of Himself, consisting of our spirit, within us at creation then we too would be divine. There shall forever be a clear distinction between Creator and creation. The distinction will largely be defined by the fact that God has always been and we have not. Our spirit and soul were created eternal and are not infinite as is God. Our spirit is not a piece of God, and neither is it an extension of God. Moreover, God cannot create a person and they become as if they had always existed. In other words, God cannot duplicate Himself but He can create after His image. On the sixth day, "...God created man in His own image (Genesis 1:27, 31). Man was created wholly human at that time—spirit, soul, and body (1 Thessalonians 5:23).

The whole counsel of Scripture does not teach that God put part of Himself into us at creation, and neither does it teach that we will at some point in eternity become divine.

Someone might respond to this statement with the following point:

"What about where the book of the Revelation (21:22) speaks of the Lamb being the temple and yet we know that God's people comprise the temple?"

Let me say this again, yet more clearly. In order to be divine then we would have to measure up to the attributes of its definition. To be divine requires our having *never* been created. Truthfully and conclusively, there is no way to get around the fact that we are created beings. It is clear in the book of The Revelation that one of the theme songs before God's throne lauds Him as Creator and we are revealed as those who are created for His pleasure (The Revelation 4:11). When we see Him as He is, then we will clearly understand why the hosts of Heaven fall down, worship Him, and end their worship with "forever and ever" (The Revelation 5:13; 7:12). This reveals the deepest longing of creation and the reason for our being created—to worship Him forever and ever. There is a desperate need in all of God's creation to hail Him as the Creator. This will continue throughout all of eternity. There is no indication that this order will or can change. In fact, Lucifer attempted to disrupt this order and was expelled from Heaven (Isaiah 14, The Revelation 12). When we see God as He is, we will only be able to do what all the other hosts of Heaven are doing and will clearly understand that none can be God except Him. There will not be anything in us, like Lucifer, that would even attempt to "be like the Most High." We will be content with having been created solely for His pleasure. Our deepest longings will find ultimate fulfillment in worshiping Him as our God, Creator, and Redeemer forever and ever.

Recognizing Persuasive Words

The passage referred to in the point (The Revelation 21:22) gives no indication that we are or can in any way be divine. It indicates that God and the Lamb will be the temple, and that there is no need for a temple *edifice* when you are standing before the One the temple is intended to represent. They are the temple and people will walk in their light (v.23). People will not walk in and out of an edifice that God and the Lamb are dwelling in. There is no indication that the temple referred to here is the body of Christ. In fact, it clearly states that *God the Father and the Lamb are the temple.*

There are other passages of Scripture in the New Testament where reference to the "temple of God" is obviously not referring to the body of Christ. To automatically assume that such passages refer to the body of Christ would be at least presumptuous. For example, in Hebrews 9, the writer reveals that the Old Testament tabernacle or temple was a "copy" of the heavenly original. This indicates that there is a literal heavenly temple that verse 23 refers to as a "heavenly thing." A "thing" is not a person or a group of people. There is obviously a literal heavenly temple and the time will come, according to The Revelation 21:22, when it will not be necessary. The use of the word "temple" in Scripture does not always refer to the Church.

The roots of anti-Semitism in the Church can be, in part, traced back to people making this same dreadful error. While the Bible does teach that the Church, consisting of both Jew and Gentile, is spiritual Israel, that does not support our interpreting the name "Israel" in all of its instances in the New Testament as being the Church. Where Scripture states that "all of Israel will be saved" (Romans 11:26), it is clear that Paul is referring to the nation. The problem is that some people try to interpret "Israel" in this passage when it needs no interpretation. When read in its context, it becomes quite clear to whom Paul was referring.

In Romans 11:1, Paul refers to himself as being an Israelite of the tribe of Benjamin and then continues to expound on God's dealings with that nation throughout the rest of the chapter. The people of the "Israel" that shall be saved (v.26) are revealed as the "natural branches" (v.21), contrasted with the Gentile nations (v.25), and identified as enemies for the gospels sake (v.28). These descriptions perfectly fit *the nation* of Israel. Can it be any clearer than that as to whom Paul was referring? All of Romans 9-11 reveals God's redemptive plan in dealing with the nation of Israel and the Gentiles. It reveals that God is not finished with the nation of Israel because of His promises to Abraham. Read it for yourself. Understand also that there will always be those who will believe what they want to in spite of all the evidence.

To further illustrate, Matthew 20:17 states: "Now Jesus, going up to Jerusalem, took the twelve disciples aside on the road and said to them..." To which Jerusalem was Jesus going? The New Jerusalem in Heaven? If we read further we will find that it is the earthly Jerusalem in which He was to be crucified. *The only reason a person would let such spiritual common sense escape them in interpreting Scripture is because of having preconceived ideas. They already have a biased or influenced viewpoint concerning the matter.* Their bias is evidence that they have already given themselves over to the spirit of error even though they may call it "revelation."

What about in the Old Testament where it states: "Out of Egypt I have called My son" (Hosea 11:1). The word "son" was obviously referring to Israel when read in its context, but Matthew 2:15 states that Christ fulfilled it as a child when He and His parents came back from Egypt. Obviously, Matthew was prompted by the Holy Spirit to draw this parallel. There are many spiritual parallels when comparing the Old with the New Testament. These parallels are not necessarily considered prophecy, but, nevertheless, are prophetic in nature. The life of Joseph, King David, and many others all resemble in varying ways Christ's life on earth. In fact, Jesus taught that there would be many ways in which our lives as Christians would resemble His in works, sufferings, and blessings. In a sense, we would also be fulfilling what Christ did on earth by doing likewise. However, our doing those things does not take away from the fact that He did them. The fact is that Israel was called out of Egypt and so was Christ. It would be erroneous for me to say the Scripture was only referring to Christ. The Holy Spirit will prompt us to see spiritual parallels in Scripture, history, and current events. This is quite different from ignoring the facts and drawing conclusions that are entirely contrary to the facts. The fact is that The Revelation 21:22 states that God and the Lamb are the temple, not the Church, and Romans 11:26 is clearly, beyond argument, referring to the nation of Israel.

Drawing allegorical conclusions from Scripture that the context does not allow is *often* evidence of the spirit of error. This is why we must only interpret Scripture by revelation received from God, and to receive revelation, we cannot have any preconceived notions. If we think we are clever in interpreting Scripture, then we have been interpreting it by our cleverness and not by revelation from God and are consequently in error. We cannot make assumptions that certain words represent something other than what the context obviously states. If we do so, it is indicative of a proud or puffed up mind. Matthew did not assume that Israel's having been called out of Egypt was a precursor to a similar event in Christ's life. He was prompted by the Holy Spirit to do so. Because of our "cleverness," we will overlook the obvious and concoct "revelations" that cause people to boast in us. Remember, *anything* that originates from our logic is rooted in pride.

A lot of doctrinal error can be avoided by reading Scripture in its context. In relation to the personal application of Scripture, the Holy Spirit can make it applicable in many ways in our daily lives. Nevertheless, *there are things in Scripture that are mere fact and need or allow no interpretation.* The Holy Spirit may reveal to us spiritual parallels from such, but let us make sure that we also stay true to the context.

It would appear that the following two points imply that there is no distinction between God and us: (1) Paul referred to Christ's people as Christ when he spoke of the impudence of thinking that Christ should be joined to a harlot (1 Corinthians 6:14-20). (2) Jesus made no distinction between Himself and those who Saul persecuted (Acts 9:4).

Even though we are one spirit with Christ does not mean we become Him. When a man leaves his father and mother and cleaves to his wife, the two become one flesh (Ge nesis 2:22-24). Does that mean the man becomes the woman and the woman becomes the man, thus losing their distinctiveness? The answer to that is common knowledge. Yet, if someone mistreats or dishonors my wife they also mistreat me. The oneness between a man and his wife is a type of the oneness between the Lord and His Church (Ephesians 5). This is why Jesus asked, "Why are you persecuting Me?" when Saul was actually persecuting the Church (Acts 9:4).

"But he who is joined to the Lord is one spirit with Him" (1 Corinthians 6:17). Notice that this verse does not state that we become one personality, mind, soul, or body with the Lord but that we become *one spirit* with Him. "But we have this treasure in earthen vessels, that the excellence of the power may be of God and not of us" (2 Corinthians 4:7). We are vessels (carriers) of the treasure of God's glory on a very intimate level. This intimate level is defined by our being one with Him. Yet, as equally important, we are distinguished from Him as His vessel or temple—a carrier of the One who is the treasure. To conclude that the Lord teaches that there is no distinction between Him and us is reading into Scripture something that is not there.

Any implication in Scripture of our being "Christ" is only alluded to in a representative sense. God's purpose is that we are to be *conformed to the image* of His Son (Romans 8:29). In other words, we are to be *like* Him. When people see us, they should see Christ. When I click on an *icon* on the desktop of my computer, it causes the program, to which it is pointing, to appear on the screen. The icons on the desktop are not the actual programs, but are shortcuts to them. We are but icons pointing to the real program—Christ, and this will never change. As Paul stated, "we are ambassadors for Christ" (2 Corinthians 5:20). An ambassador represents one nation to another. Any harm done to an ambassador of a nation could be considered an act of war against the nation represented.

Conclusive truth must be revealed through the anointing that abides within us, and this anointing interprets and agrees with Scripture. While the things we conclude may sound logical, are they the product of our preconceived ideas and of the persuasiveness of men? *We can lose our bearings for the truth by naively subjecting ourselves to a spirit of error. If we boast in men, they will easily influence us.* Therefore, the conclusions we draw from Scripture must glorify the One of whom they testify—Jesus.

There are eschatological and basic doctrinal views in the body of Christ that have originated from reading into Scripture something that is not there. It is not difficult to take a preconceived idea and twist Scripture to back it up. There have also been (and still are) whole movements or sects in Christendom that based their existence on supposed "revelation" from the Lord and, nevertheless, were in error. In some cases, conclusions were made about Scripture passages that were achieved by drawing allegorical conclusions contrary to the truth and the context.

From such movements or sects have come people who claim they have received "special revelation" that no one else has. They spend a lot of time focusing on "truths" that do not really bring edification. They do this because of pride—that people might glory in their ability to get "revelation." Any revelation derived from the logic or the deductive ability of a person's intellect is at least fleshly and proud and can be demonic (James 3:13-17). The question we must ask is: do such "revelations" glorify Christ or do they draw attention to withering flesh?

The people that the devil uses to deceive others in this way are usually men or women who are genuinely of God, but at some point in their walk, they transgressed against God's ways. It is likely that a sense of elation that comes from having people look to them with awe, because of the gifts of God, became a snare as it did with Lucifer. As a minister begins to entertain and feed off of such elation, he or she begins to compromise humility and develops a subtle sense of superiority. Such deception usually cloaks the victim with false securities. More specifically, the calling, the gifts, the position of influence, and flattery becomes their source of life instead of the Lord. Understand that this diabolical work in its beginning stages is so subtle that it can go completely unrecognized. It can happen over a period of years. If it takes the devil ten years to deceive us, he will not become impatient in doing so.

Because Balaam could not, through proclamation, bring a curse on the Israelites, he taught Balak, the Moabite king, how to bring the Israelites under God's judgment (Numbers 22-25). The spirit of Balaam is at work in the Church today to deceive spiritual leaders into coming under God's judgment. If the devil cannot get them to fall for some sort of lust of the flesh, he will attempt to cunningly get them to become competitors with God for the affections and loyalty of the people. Most leaders who are deceived in this way do not know they are walking on dangerous ground.

A person who makes *unrighteous* judgments against certain sects of the Church in reference to their alleged doctrinal error or religious bondage always ends up in doctrinal error or religious bondage themselves. This holds true without exception. There are those who have condemned the spiritually bankrupt "religious system" within the Church only to end up on that same path. This is because of their not walking in love toward all. What profit is there in our condemning the way others in the body of Christ have structured their meetings, yet we do not have love in our hearts toward them?

A spiritual leader may have a clearer understanding of what true New Covenant church meetings should look like and may even allow greater freedom of expression in the meetings they oversee, but this does not mean that there is actually greater freedom. Without love, the leader and the people they oversee will become more devoted to their freedom than to Christ, and, thus their freedom becomes bondage. They will become as devoted to their "freedom" as they say others are devoted to their traditions and bondage. This has become evident in certain movements and denominations in the Church. When any movement, church, or organization becomes proud (as if their way is the best), then they step out of love into darkness, and that which they became proud of becomes a snare to them (a means of stumbling). Pride judges others as being inferior, and is the root of all the disunity that exists in the Church. It is revealed in attitudes like, "I have the truth and they don't." If you have the truth, it will not be something you will have to boast about. You will know a tree by its fruit. An apple tree proves it is an apple tree by producing apples. True revelation comes only to "babes" as expounded on in an earlier chapter. Babes only boast in the Lord—the One who is their only source of life.

> "He who loves his brother abides in the light, and there is no cause for stumbling in him. (11) But he who hates his brother is in darkness and walks in darkness, and does not know where he is going, because the darkness has blinded his eyes".
>
> (1 John 2:10-11)

Without love, we will spend more time stumbling and trying to find our way than making true advances on the path to freedom from religious bondage.

How we respond to error is just as important as the exposing and condemnation of it. To condemn error and then fail to love those who are in it will place us into darkness that will cause us to blindly stumble in a similar way to those we have judged. Our tainted ability to reason will become the master and not the ability of the Holy Spirit to impart revelation. *Our reasoning ability is a tool of the Holy Spirit and we must never allow it to become the high thing that exalts itself against the knowledge of God* (2 Corinthians 10:3-6).

While pride is the root of all spiritual error and dead religious form, we cannot be proud in our condemnation of such. All unrighteous judgment is rooted in pride or proud arguments. While one cannot conform to error or anything that is against Christ, a nonconformist mentality associated with pride will lead us in to a blind conformity to the spirit of error. Let us be careful that we do not strain out "gnats" of error and swallow "camels" of pride in judging others (Matthew 23:24). Pride is the worst error of all.

In light of all of this, it is obvious that to teach that we are or will at some point in time become divine appeals to the pride of life in man. Remember what the serpent (Lucifer) said to Eve in the Garden, "...you shall be as God, knowing good and evil" (Genesis 3:5). This was similar to the self-deception that he had completely embraced. Listen to his delusions of grandeur:

> "I will ascend into heaven, I will exalt my throne above the stars of God: I will sit on the mount of the congregation, on

the farthest sides of the north; (14) I will ascend above the heights of the clouds; I will be like the Most High".

(Isaiah 14:13-14)

The Most High interrupted Lucifer's self-destructive foolishness with:

"Yet [in spite of what you boast] you shall be brought down to Sheol, to the lowest depths of the Pit".

(v.15)

The goal of the spirit of error is to twist the truth of God, thus creating an illusive way that exalts man without him having to humble himself under God's hand. This deceptive way is of the spirit of antichrist at work in the world today (1 John 4:1-6). This spirit seeks to get us to replace a dependency on the inherent witness of the Holy Spirit with knowledge from another source. As the result, this will keep us from abiding in Christ, and we will eventually seek to draw life from things that only minister death. We will not realize that it is death because of the spiritually numbing effect that the following have over us: the fear, praise, and acceptance of men and the prestige of belonging to the "greatest" or the doctrinally "purest" church or organization.

Our sinful flesh will attempt in many ways to escape the way of the cross. It finds the devil's seductive lies very appealing.

"There is a way that seems right to a man, but its end is the way of death".

(Proverbs 14:12)

Jesus told of those who would try to climb up some other (illusive) way to enter the sheepfold instead of coming through Him—the Door. He said they were thieves and robbers and that they come only to steal, kill, and destroy (John 10:1-11). This path can eventually lead to destruction as it did with the Jews in 70 A.D. when the Roman General Titus massacred one million of them and destroyed Jerusalem and the temple. This fulfilled the judgment that Christ pronounced over them for not receiving Him (See Matthew 23:34-39).

Jesus told His disciples concerning certain Jews:

> "They shall put you out of the synagogues; yes, the time is coming that whoever kills you will think that he offers God service".
>
> (John 16:2)

In conclusion, a person can be entirely convinced that what they believe and are doing is of God, and, instead, be antichrist or hostile to the true anointing of God and His anointed ones. Let us be careful to know why we believe what we believe—a people who do not need to be ashamed and who stay off the broad way to destruction.

Modern Day Apparitions

There are those who allege that Mary, the mother of Jesus, and Jesus have been appearing to them. It was reported that Mary was appearing to some and telling them, among other things, to follow Jesus. Then later, Jesus started appearing. This sounds quite persuasive and is definitely a type of experience with which I am not familiar. However, one must ask:

Would or can Jesus and Mary appear to someone on earth today?

Jesus appeared to Saul (Paul) on the Road to Damascus but there was no mention of Mary (Acts 9:1-7). In fact, the only time God allowed someone on earth to speak to the dead was when Samuel appeared to King Saul when he went to the witch of En Dor for guidance (1 Samuel 28:7-25). Such things were forbidden by the Lord (Leviticus 20:27; Deuteronomy 18:11), but in this case, the Lord intervened and sent Samuel to rebuke Saul. Mary is dead but Jesus is risen and alive for evermore. Scripture in no way exalts Mary, the mother of Jesus, to the status of a mediator between God and humanity. For there is one God and one Mediator between God and men, the Man Christ Jesus (1 Timothy 2:5).

Although an apparition of "Mary" was telling people to follow "Jesus," was she still receiving the adoration of the people and was she the center of attention? *Anything* that draws our hearts away from God to something else is not of Him. Did such appearances cause people to venerate God or the apparitions? The devil is crafty enough to get people to believe they are worshiping God, even while they are committing idolatry. Just because someone who calls herself "Mary" appears to us and tells us to follow "Jesus" does not validate it as being of God. Remember that the devil can appear as an angel of light. We must be careful that we do not judge such things according to outward appearance or be influenced by the persuasive words we hear.

> "Beloved, do not believe every spirit, but test the spirits, whether they are of God; because many false prophets have gone out into the world".
>
> (1 John 4:1)

John continues and reveals three decisive factors that prove whether a person or spirit is of God:

1. They must confess that Jesus Christ has come in the flesh (v. 3), and that He is the Son of God (v.15). The Word became flesh, dwelt among us, and the Word was God (John 1:1, 14). Jesus in the flesh is as much human as He is divine. He is the Son of Man *and* the Son of God. Anyone teaching contrary to this is not of God. Anyone who would attempt to exalt themselves or some one else to this status is not of God.
2. Do they speak as those of the world and do those of the world listen to them (v. 5)? Those who are of the world only hear what is appealing to the lust of the flesh, the lust of the eyes, and the pride of life (1 John 2:16-17). Where does their authority originate from, and what means of influence are they using? Do they refuse to hear and teach the truth (v. 6)?
3. Is there evidence of God's love? Those who love and

speak the truth will have God's love coming from their hearts (vs. 7, 8, 20). They will diffuse the "aroma" of Christ. His selflessness, meekness, and lowliness will be the most evident things about them.

In summary, those of God's creation who are truly submitted to His authority will glorify Christ alone. The only way to do this is by the Holy Spirit who only glorifies Jesus (1 Corinthians 12:3; John 16:13-14). If it smells, looks, tastes, and acts like Jesus then it is of God. We will know what He smells, looks, tastes, and acts like only if we are abiding in Him by the teaching of the anointing within us.

> "But even if we, or an angel from heaven, preach any other gospel unto you than what we have preached to you, let him be accursed".
> (Galatians 1:8)

Free from the Law or Lawless?

What if someone told you that since we are not under the law anymore, then we can do whatever we want? How would you respond? What if they quoted the following Scripture passage?

> "All things are lawful for me, but not all things are helpful...".
> (1 Corinthians 10:23; See also 6:12)

First, understand that Paul also said in 1 Corinthians 9:19, 21, "I have made myself a servant to all ... to those who are without law, as without law (not being without law toward God, but under law toward Christ), that I might win those who are without law..."

Paul clearly states that we are still under law toward Christ. In other words, we are not our own because Jesus purchased us with His blood (1 Corinthians 6:20; 7:23). We have a new Master or Lord.

We are under the dominion of grace (Romans 6:14), and it teaches us to deny ungodliness and worldly lusts (Titus 2:11-12).

In addition, the definition of the word "all" as it is used in 1 Corinthians 6:12 and 10:23 does not indicate "everything" or "everyone" in many of its uses in the New Testament. It can also be defined as *"some of all kinds."* Paul was saying that many things were lawful for him but not everything (1 Corinthians 6:12 & 10:23). He knew who his Lord and Master was and lived his life to serve Him and not himself (1 Corinthians 9:19-21). To believe or teach that Jesus promotes our having "freedom to sin" is a dreadful error and promotes self-will and rebellion.

Did Jesus Suffer in Hell?

Does this sound persuasive? Since we deserve the torment of eternal separation from God because of the inherited sin nature and the fact that we have all sinned and have been found guilty by God, it was necessary for Jesus to suffer in Hell for us so that we would not have to. When the Father forsook the Son on the cross, Jesus spiritually died in our behalf. Are these statements true or false according to God's purposes? They are persuasive, they make sense, and seem to be logical, yet there is one big problem. The law, the prophets, Jesus, and the apostles never taught any such doctrine. Search the Scriptures yourself and find out. The Bible does say that Jesus went into Hell but says nothing about Him suffering there (Acts 2:25-28). In the Old Testament, "Sheol" was obviously the abode of the dead—of both the righteous and the unrighteous. *Paradise* or what some have referred to as *Abraham's Bosom* was located there along with the place of punishment for the unrighteous. A large gulf obviously separated the two places (see Luke 16:19-31 & 23:43). Scripture does not teach that Jesus spiritually died either. Being divine in spirit, He could not have died in that manner. 1 Peter 3:18 clearly states that Jesus was put to death *in the flesh*. This indicates a natural death but says nothing about a spiritual death.

There are many passages in which the writers of the New Testament could have mentioned the necessity of Jesus suffering in

Recognizing Persuasive Words

Hell or spiritually having to die for our redemption, but they did not (Roman 5:9; Ephesians 1:7; Colossians 1:14; 1 Timothy 2:5-6; Hebrews 9:12, 15). All such passages point to Jesus' suffering on the cross (the blood) as what God required for our redemption. Anyone can twist a passage of Scripture to fit a preconceived idea. Therefore, all truth or doctrine must be consistent with the whole counsel of Scripture.

So, does Scripture state that Jesus had to die spiritually in order for us to be redeemed from spiritual death? No, in fact, all Scripture points to His physical death as being what God required. A look into some passages in the book of Hebrews will settle the issue.

"He [Jesus] then would have had to suffer often since the foundation of the world; but now, once in the end of the ages, He has appeared to put away sin BY THE SACRIFICE of Himself" (9:26). Chapter 10:5-12 further states, (5) "Therefore, when he came into the world, He said, 'Sacrifice and offering you did not desire, BUT A BODY You have prepared for me. (6) In burnt offerings and sacrifices for sin You had no pleasure.' (7) Then said I, 'Behold, I have come - in the volume of the book it is written of me - to do Your will, O God.' (8) Previously saying, 'Sacrifice and offering, burnt offerings, and offering for sin You did not desire, nor had pleasure in them' (which are offered according to the law), (9) then He said, 'Behold, I have come to do Your will, O God.' He takes away the first that he may establish the second. (10) By that will we have been sanctified THROUGH THE OFFERING OF THE BODY of Jesus Christ ONCE FOR ALL. (11) And every priest stands ministering daily and offering repeatedly the same sacrifices, which can never take away sins. (12) But this Man, after he had offered one sacrifice for sins forever, sat down at the right hand of God" (emphasis mine).

Jesus agreed to come into the world and do the will of God. That "will" is identified in the preceding passages as *the offering of the body that His Father prepared for Him* (vv. 5, 9, 10). Note that it did not include Him suffering in Hell or dying spiritually. The suffering that Jesus was to go through was only while he was in his body. The death that He suffered was to only be while in His body.

When Jesus put away or abolished sin by His bodily sacrifice (9:26), there was also a setting aside of the punishment required by God's justice. *Where there is no sin, there is no need for punishment.* It would be a great injustice if the judicial courts of our land punished a man for crimes of which they could find no evidence. Without the evidence of a crime having been committed, there would be no place for punishment. How much more just is God? Jesus' death on the cross did away with all the evidence of our sin. For this reason, He did not have to suffer in Hell for us or spiritually die. He gave himself, His body, on the cross as a ransom for all (1 Timothy 2:5, 6). As He said before He died, "It is finished" (John 19:30). He did not say, "To be continued." In saying that, He indicated that He had fulfilled what the law and the prophets (the whole counsel of Scripture) required for our redemption. The debt was paid in full at the cross.

The Apostle Paul declared that the message of the *cross* is the power of God unto salvation and that he sought to know nothing except Jesus Christ and Him *crucified* (1 Corinthians 1:18-24 & 2:2; Romans 1:16). Notice that he did not include Christ suffering in Hell as part of the message.

As we have just read, Scripture reveals that God required a bodily sacrifice for redemption from sin. Jesus offered one sacrifice (His body) one time for all people, and then sat down at God's right hand. His suffering was complete in that one offering, or the need for further suffering would have been mentioned.

Now, did I add anything into Scripture that is not there? Did I twist something to make it say what I wanted it to? Did what I said agree with the whole counsel of Scripture? I think you know the answer to that.

Someone might respond, "Why should it matter what you believe concerning the issue?" The Apostle Paul answered that:

> "...That your faith should not stand in the wisdom of men but in the power of God".
>
> (1 Corinthians 2:5)

If we are putting faith in the persuasive words and teachings of men, then our faith is powerless and vain. 1 Corinthians 1:17 forcefully states that the message of the cross is made of no effect by "wise" words that come from men. If you want to know the full power of the cross in your life, I would suggest you not believe that Jesus suffered in Hell or that He died spiritually.

Do you see how being overly devoted to or fond of a minister or organization and their teachings can keep us from maturing in Christ by hindering our spiritual discernment? Is it now clearer to you, that what you believe can affect your spiritual discernment, and that we must correctly interpret Scripture? Is it clear that we cannot allow any teaching from any man or spirit (no matter how reputable they are) to replace the teaching of the inherent anointing that abides within us? This anointing is true, does not lie, will teach us concerning all truth, and by it we will abide in Him who is the Truth (1 John 2:27). It will keep us and unite us as one until He comes to gather us to Himself.

Remember, beloved of the Lord, that you have all things and need not boast in men. This includes the ability to know Him intimately through the Holy Scriptures.

Oh Father, purify our hearts. Deliver us from division, and unite us that we may see Your glory upon the Church. Father, may Your people love and value the Truth more than life itself, more than all the riches of the world combined. Free us from our self-made prisons of sectarianism that hold us captive to the fear and praise of man.

Lord, reveal any areas in our lives where we depend more upon our rationale, a minister, church, or organization, than upon our God-given ability to discern You and the teachings of the Bible. Keep us from being overly fond of or attached to any person to the degree that they replace the Holy Spirit in our lives. In the name of Your most wonderful and beloved Son, Jesus, we ask. Amen.

Truths in Review

1. It is not important what we believe doctrinally. We should just make sure that we all get along in the body of Christ. True or False? Why or why not?

2. What did the people who Jesus taught say that He had that the scribes did not have. Why did Jesus have it and the scribes not have it?
3. What is the clear difference between those who speak by revelation from God and as His mouthpiece, and those who speak from themselves? What does Scripture say about those who speak from themselves?
4. Why did the religious leaders of Jesus' day reject Him even though they were looking and longing for the Messiah? Why did they not discern it was Him?
5. Is it possible for a Christian to be deceived by the persuasive words of another? Name some scenarios in which this could happen. Has it happened to you?
6. What state of mind serves as the catalyst for God's people to boast in and wrongly relate to spiritual leaders?
7. In what ways is the church in America similar to the church in Corinth in reference to our relationship to spiritual leaders? (1 Corinthians 1-3)
8. In whom does the Bible say that there is no darkness at all?
9. Can you, in your own words, describe the process that the devil uses to get us to turn "off" the inherent witness of the Spirit and give ourselves over to the spirit of error?
10. Can you think of some instances where you know you came face to face with the spirit of error?
11. Can you think of some teachings that you have been introduced to that should be categorized as persuasive words of men? Can you Biblically explain why they are erroneous?
12. Since Scripture reveals that we are the temple of God, then it would be safe to assume that the use of the word "temple" in the New Testament always refers to us. True or False? Why or why not?
13. To condemn error and then fail to love those who are in it will place us into darkness that will cause us to

Recognizing Persuasive Words

blindly stumble in a similar way to those we have judged. True or False? Why or why not?
14. What is the worst error of all and how does it affect our perception of others? (All unrighteous judgments come from this.)
15. Pride is the source of all the disunity in the Church? True or false? Why or why not?
16. Not all things that originate from our logic are rooted in pride. True or false? Why or why not?
17. How would you biblically respond, if you heard someone teach that we, the Church, are the Israel of God, that God has completely rejected the nation of Israel, that He will never deal with them again, and gave you Scripture to support their view?
18. The Spirit of truth always, without exception, glorifies Christ? True or false?
19. If someone (i.e. a human or angel) tells us they were sent by God but allows us to fall down in adoration of them without rebuking us and instructing us to worship God the Father and the Lord Jesus Christ, then they are not of God. True or false?
20. What could happen to us if our faith is in the persuasive words of men and not in the power of God?

Part Five

Seeing God with a Pure Heart

Our heart must be purified in order to develop spiritual discernment. As our heart becomes purer, our spiritual vision will become clearer.

> "To the pure all things are pure, but to those who are defiled and unbelieving nothing is pure; but even their mind and conscience are defiled".
>
> (Titus 1:15)

The defilement of sin will cause us to perceive all things, including people, God, and the things of God, through its filter. Even that which is pure would not be valued for what it is because of such defilement. *It would be used for selfish gain instead.* To what degree do we serve God for selfish reasons? Do we have a need to be heard or seen? Are we drawn to "the ministry" because it appeals to our self-esteem? What are our motives in relation to the things of God? The reason we do not find favor with God in some areas of our lives can be attributed, to a large degree, to impure motives.

When Adam and Eve ate from the tree of the knowledge of good and evil, darkness covered their hearts, and they lost the ability to judge or discern righteously. Adam blamed Eve out of fear and insecurity because the point of reference for relating to God and one another had been reduced to an independent knowledge of or information about good and evil. A defiled conscience became the standard and not the love of God. Adam and Eve only retained a vague impression of what they had before and could no longer see or discern God or one another rightly. Sin's defilement caused them to hide from and turn away from looking into God's glory. *The darkness of their insecurity replaced the standard and full assurance of His love.*

> "Blessed are the pure in heart, for they shall see God".
> (Matthew 5:8)

Conscience is a function of the heart of man (Hebrews 10:22). From it, he gets the ability to distinguish good from evil. It also gives him the ability to see (perceive), discern, or distinguish God. Conscience was never made to function apart from Him. As long as it maintains its gaze upon the Lord, His love will remain its point of reference, first in judging our lives, and then others. Consequently, we will know the reality of His love shed abroad in our hearts by the Holy Spirit (Romans 5:5). The blood of the Lamb of God who takes away the sins of the world commands the undivided attention of the impure conscience of humanity to look longingly into the glory of God and find refuge and peace. The pure conscience looks into the glory of God as revealed in the Gospel and mirrors what it sees, thus transforming the person and then others (2 Corinthians 3:18). Our conscience inhabited by the Holy Spirit (the one who lavishly sheds the love of God in our hearts) is the anointing or the witness of the Spirit referred to in chapter one of this book.

> "Therefore, brethren, having boldness to enter the Holiest by the blood of Jesus, (20) by a new and living way which He consecrated for us, through the veil, that is, His flesh, (21) and having a High Priest over the house of God, (22) let us draw near with a TRUE [sincere] HEART in full assurance of faith, having our HEARTS sprinkled from an EVIL CONSCIENCE and our bodies washed with pure water".
> (Hebrews 10:19-22; emphasis mine)

CHAPTER FIFTEEN

Discernment: An Extension of Love

"And this I pray, that your love may abound still more and more in knowledge and all discernment, (10) that you may approve the things that are excellent, and that you may be sincere and without offense until the Day of Christ, (11) being filled with the fruits of righteousness which are by Jesus Christ, to the glory and praise of God"
(Philippians 1:9-11)

This passage of Scripture clearly states that knowledge and discernment are to be an extension of God's love through us. The knowledge referred to here is of our love developing into an intimate relationship of knowing the Lord. The discernment referred to is the intuitive ability acquired by our becoming intimately joined with Him. The love that we receive from Him will become the means that enables us to discern our fellow man correctly. Consequently, we will see the darkness in people's hearts and give light, life, and hope. The light of God's love will set the captives free like a sword, cutting through hardness and deception. This kind of love will not tolerate darkness but exposes and reproves it and also heals and brings reconciliation where needed.

This knowledge and discernment according to the above Scripture passage will also keep us "... sincere and without offense until the Day of Christ." The word "sincere" is defined: "Found pure when unfolded and examined by the sun's light." The phrase "without offense" can be defined: "To be blameless in not being troubled by a consciousness of sin or in not leading others into sin by our example."

If we walk in the light as Jesus is in the light, we will find it unnecessary to attempt to cover our sin tracks. Only the Lord can cover our spiritual nakedness. It is impossible to find spiritual covering inherent within people. Those who have allowed themselves to be sincere (completely spiritually vulnerable or naked) before God will be sincere before men. As the result, there will be no room for offense because then, and only then, will we perceive one another correctly. If we are sincere, then we will recognize any insincerity within others, thus causing us to know what to expect from them. There will be no impurity in us that will lead others astray. Even if there is impurity, that would not matter to those who are truly sincere because of their willingness to deal with it before God.

The tendency to be insincere and run and hide came from the fall of Adam. Man has bought into the lie that only in hiding will he be protected and secure. Yet, our failure to trust God's remedy will only secure our demise. Let us look to His remedy—Jesus' death on the cross—and live. To be sincere is to be fully convinced that the only safe and secure place is in God's unmerited grace and that it is our only hope.

The sincere person will walk in love and will not be an offense or stumblingblock to others. This would entail not looking for what is wrong with them. This is a major offense in the Church today. People do not need us to be a "walking Ten Commandments" to them, but they need Jesus. We are to minister Him to them, and not a standard of right and wrong, because Jesus is the standard. His Gospel is the message as opposed to a knowledge of good and evil. He will bring the necessary conviction in people's hearts if we allow Him to be revealed through us. Those who truly know Him as the only source of life will not minister those things that bring death and cause many to stumble (2 Corinthians 3).

Discernment: An Extension of Love

Prophecy:

"The time is at hand when I, the Lord, will no longer endure in the sacred assembly the offerings of Cain that are continuously presented before Me. He offered his best, and yet it was not what I required. He offered it with an insincere heart and not with a true heart. Those who come before Me must do so as one who is naked, as one who is not trusting in his accomplishments, ingenuity, and cleverness. Many of your covering garments are not of Me. You trust more in the works of your own hands. You cover yourself with futility and call it godly service. You cover yourself with self-righteousness and call it My righteousness. If I would not accept strange fire in the Old Testament, do you think that I will accept in the New? The only offerings that are accepted by My Father are those that bear the aroma of My suffering on the cross. These bear the aroma of My love for all people.

The fire that I am about to send to My Church will set in order that which is out of order. This is My order: those who worship Me must do so in Spirit and in truth. The Spirit and truth all point to My suffering on the cross. This fire will be the truth set aflame by My Holy Spirit that will burn away the refuge of lies, false humility, and religious disguises that My people have covered themselves with. You will know then that it is truly a fearful thing to fall into the hands of the living God. Yet, at the same time you will know that it is the safest and most secure place one could possibly be. In My hands, your iniquities will be purged and you will be clothed from on High.

After my people have known My goodness and severity and mercy and judgments, then these same things can be established in the earth. Through these shall the knowledge of the glory of the Lord fill the earth as the waters cover the sea."

CHAPTER SIXTEEN

Grace and Truth

"And the Word became flesh and dwelt among us, and we beheld His glory, the glory as of the only Begotten of the Father, full of grace and truth".

(John 1:14)

John saw Christ as being *full of* grace and truth. Truth was Christ's standard and grace was His motivation. The truth reveals our need for freedom from sin, and grace provides the means. Truth without grace is religious legalism, and grace without truth is a license to self-will and rebellion. Truth demands complete surrender to Christ's Lordship, and grace constrains and enables us to trust in and willingly surrender to it. Combined, they establish God's righteousness within the heart of man. Jesus always spoke the truth with grace, and He never showed grace apart from truth. *When we look into God's glory this is what we will see: Jesus, full of grace and truth.*

When Christ confronted the darkness in people, He would always respond with grace and truth. The union of grace and truth defines the love of Christ and are the essential ingredients to developing spiritual discernment. We must believe in the power of God's love to change people much more than the faith we put in our ability recognize and point out what is wrong in people, thinking that will change them. God's love will distinguish, expose, convict, deliver, heal, and reconcile. Do you truly believe in its power?

I have seen the power of God's love at work. I have seen it melt the hardest of hearts and cut through the fiercest resistance to the Holy Spirit. It heals the worst of diseases and strengthens the hearts of men. It calms the troubled emotions and arrests the worst of pain. It delivers the most tormented minds and liberates the captives of sin. Oh, beloved of God, cease to take refuge in those things that are lies—those things that can only provide false security. Come out of the shadows into the Light from whom nothing is hidden. Let the refuge of Christ's love be the anchor of your soul. God has provided all that you need. He will not shame you, but He will cause you to see your true self. In that place, you will find the grace to rise as a new creation in Christ.

Oh, if only we would grasp the need for Jesus, full of grace and truth, to be revealed through us. We would never be the same. Ministry as we have known it would be revolutionized. Preaching good sermons would no longer be the focus. We would no longer have to "pull teeth" to motivate the people of God for they will be volunteers in the day of His power (Psalm 110:1-3). We have had the days of good sermonizing. Now it is time for the day of God's power. Some of the best preachers and teachers in the world are from America, but we see very little transformation and revival. Oh, how the ministers of our day need Jesus Christ Himself to be expressed and revealed through their words. When He fills the substance of our words, then the people will meet Jesus and not the personality, emotions, or intellect of a human. They will never be the same again.

Dearest Father, baptize us anew in Your love so that we may see as You see. Purify our hearts so that we may look steadfastly into Your glory. We are desperate for You. Let every area where we have wrongly judged Your people be revealed to us. If we have failed to reveal Jesus as full of grace and truth, then give us the ability to do so. Amen.

Truths in Review

1. True spiritual discernment is the intuitive ability we

Grace and Truth

attain from having the love of God in our hearts. True or false?
2. What Scripture passage reveals this more clearly than any other?
3. The "Ten Commandments" are the points of reference for all true spiritual discernment. True or False. If not, then what is?
4. What is the definition of the word "sincere" used in Philippians 1:9-11?
5. What happened to Adam and Eve's spiritual discernment after eating of the Tree of the Knowledge of Good and Evil?
6. What has greater influence in the way *you* presently judge others: the love of Christ or the Tree of the Knowledge of Good and Evil?
7. What cleanses our hearts (consciences) so that we can clearly discern and reflect the glory of God?
8. In what ways, in your Christian walk, have you put more faith in your ability to recognize and point out what is wrong in other people rather than in power of God's love to change them?
9. What are the two essential ingredients needed to develop spiritual discernment?
10. What significance does the fact that Jesus is full of grace and truth have in the way we relate to others?
11. In what way is this an indictment against religious legalism and license to sin?

Part Six

Some Final Guidelines on Discernment

"My son, if you receive my words, and treasure my commands within you, (2) so that you incline your ear to wisdom, and apply your heart to understanding; (3) yes, if you cry out for discernment, and lift up your voice for understanding, (4) if you seek her as silver, and search for her as for hidden treasures; (5) then you will understand the fear of the Lord, and find the knowledge of God".

(Proverbs 2:1-5)

CHAPTER SEVENTEEN

Words for the Wise

The wise will not fellowship with those who have critical, fault-finding, and judgmental attitudes toward others. Listening to or becoming a "sounding board" for such people will mar your ability to discern correctly. Our ability to submit to and receive from a spiritual leader or anyone else in the body of Christ will be hindered if we entertain unrighteous judgments against them. There are biblical ways to deal with those who are in error in leadership.

While at Christ for the Nations Institute, I was introduced, by another student, to a book that came against various well-known leaders in the Church. A number of names were mentioned. Two well-known ministers endorsed this same book. Unfortunately, both of them became more harsh and condemning in their preaching. Eventually, one fell into sexual sin and now has only a semblance of the ministry he had before.

After reading the book, I became cynical toward the ministers accused in it. The reason for this was spiritual naivety, and, consequently, the information in the book became ammunition that I used against the accused ministers. It affected how I perceived them. Every time I heard certain words from various preachers, especially on the subjects of prosperity and faith, I would shut down my spirit from receiving what they had to say. I was also drawn to writings or teachings against them. Thank God, He opened my eyes to see how the book influenced me and showed me I was wrong in my attitude toward those accused ministers. I learned first hand that we must be careful to know the spirit behind what we read and hear from anyone.

If a spiritual leader teaches on money and prosperity, does that mean they are greedy and are trying to manipulate you to get your money? Suppose a minister makes a statement similar to, "I believe the Lord is telling me that there are 10 people in this place who can each give one thousand dollars." Does that mean they are greedy? Could it be that the Lord did tell the minister that? Could the minister say that with pure motives? Could it be that the Lord desires to bless those who would give the thousand dollars and He is using the minister to motivate them to do so? Could it be that our attributing impure motives to certain spiritual leaders stems from impure motives in our hearts? If we do not have a proper affinity with money and possessions then we could misperceive how others relate to it.

While it is dangerous to make anything the central focus besides the Lord, we must understand that even Christ taught on the subjects of money, material possessions, and how we should relate to them. One can teach on such things and still keep the people's focus on the Lord and their motives pure. However, it is true that any teaching that would move us from a place of *contentment* with the Lord and *His provision* to setting our hearts on ("bigger and better") material possessions and such is not of God. We are to be content with *the Lord's provision* for us.

We must be able to differentiate between a cynical or skeptical demonic spirit and true discernment. In this context, a cynic is someone who attributes selfish or wrong motives to all people that he or she has placed under a certain biased label or category in their thinking and belief system. A skeptic is similar in meaning and is someone who spends more time biasly questioning instead of truly believing. A cynical or skeptical state of mind is loveless and will always prevent us from grasping and receiving the truth, especially from those who we say are in error. Those who entertain a cynical or skeptical spirit toward certain spiritual leaders and movements will always end up in dire need of what they have come against. Yet, they will not be able to attain it because the darkness has blinded their eyes. Unless they repent, the result could be disastrous.

Let us take a moment a pray together. You fill in the blank with whomever it would pertain to, whether it is people, churches, or organizations.

Father, forgive me for being skeptical and cynical of _____. I do not want to be judged as I have judged them. Forgive me for agreeing with books and teachings that promote such. I command this cynical and skeptical spirit to leave me now. Thank you Father for washing me thoroughly and setting me free in Jesus' name. Amen.

Always remember that like spirits attract. Make sure that your association with others is not based on a faultfinding, judgmental, and critical spirit. For example, some have been hurt or disappointed by those in authority. We must make sure we are not drawn to them because of having been hurt accordingly. How you relate to authority plays a major role in determining whether you have true authority before God.

No accusation is to be brought against Church leadership or anyone unless there are two or three witnesses (Matthew 18:16; 1 Timothy 5:19). In any case, one must know the motivating force behind the accusations. Are the accusers spiritual and do they have a true spirit of meekness according to Galatians 6:1? Miriam and Aaron came against Moses, but God rose to his defense against them because of Moses' meekness and because they were in error (Numbers 12:1-15). Moses did not arise to his own defense. Just because a number of "reputable" people have a complaint against someone does not make it legitimate in God's eyes. Be careful about siding with anyone against someone else for any reason. Ask God to show you the true motives of those involved.

> "You shall not circulate a false report [this would include anything unsubstantiated]. Do not put your hand with the wicked to be an unrighteous witness. (2) You shall not follow a crowd to do evil; nor shall you testify in a dispute so as to turn aside after many to pervert justice".
> (Exodus 23:1-2)

Again it is written, "You shall not revile God, nor curse a ruler of your people" (Exodus 22:28), and the Apostle Paul declared, "Remind them to be subject to rulers and authorities, to obey, to be ready for every good work, (2) to speak evil of NO ONE, to be peaceable, gentle, showing humility to ALL men" (Titus 3:1-2; emphasis mine).

Every complaint that we may have against a brother must be resolved with that brother alone. If that does not resolve it, then you go to a true church elder. Do not go spreading it around to every ear that will listen. This will keep your heart pure and your spiritual vision clear.

Never leave a church, ministry, or place of employment with the wrong attitude. Young adults should never leave their parents like this either. How you perceive your previous encounter with authority will determine how you perceive the next, unless you repent. Such unresolved issues could eventually take us into a place of isolation and bitterness. Go back to those who have wronged you and those you have wronged and do all that is possible to make things right. You may find out that the way you perceived things are not the way they really are. The accuser of the brethren will use against us any unhealed hurts, unforgiveness, resentments, complaints, disappointments, unmet expectations, and regrets that we are holding on to against those in authority or anyone else, making it easier for us to believe things that are not entirely true about them.

Many of us go through life asking, "Who can I trust?" instead of asking, "For whom can I lay down my life?" This is because we are looking at people through the lenses of our past hurts. Those who walk in love do not make trust the issue. They make loving people as Jesus would the issue. This is our protection from hurt and any person like Judas that may be encountered. Moreover, *those who walk in love will not confuse suspicions that are born out of distrust, hurt, insecurity, unmet expectations, and self-righteousness with true discernment.*

Fervent Love

The Lord has made it clear that we must love one another "fervently," as commanded in 1 Peter 4:8. Any thing short of this will leave the door open to the accuser. When I hear the word "fervent," I am reminded of boiling water. There is an intensity and consistency of love that binds us together and keeps out the works of the accuser. He seeks to steal, kill, and destroy: to *steal* our peace, joy, and satisfaction in the Lord, to *kill* our influence or authority, and to *destroy* our testimony and credibility.

Peter further stated that such a love would "cover the multitude of sins." In other words, when we have this love we will have NO desire to find fault with one another, and this is proved by our actions, not just by our words. Ham, the son of Noah, was cursed because of not being quick to cover his father's physical nakedness. Instead, he went and told his two brothers (Genesis 9:20-27). Should we not, therefore, be quick to cover one another's spiritual nakedness and slow to tell others about it?

Any legitimate fault that is found with another must be kept within the confines of our relationship with them and MUST NOT be discussed behind someone's back. To do so is a grievous sin! It is sowing discord and division and is slandering a person's character. Whether we have "good intentions" and what we would call "legitimate concern" is beside the point. Intentions that *appear* to be the noblest have been used for the devil's purposes.

Peter intended well when he tried to prevent Jesus from going to Jerusalem and dying. Yet, Jesus rebuked him sharply and let him know that he was allowing the devil to use him. He had become an instrument of the devil and did not even know it. We would probably be offended if the Lord called our "good intentions" demonic. So, we must know what spirit we are of and make sure that we are not drawn in to discussion's that tear down other people.

Again, like spirits attract, and you will reap what you sow. The same standard that you use to judge others will be the standard by which others will judge you (Matthew 7). If you have a critical, faultfinding, judgmental spirit, you will be drawn to those who do also and justify such as being "genuine concern" or "good intentions." Eventually, you will start devouring one another. Remember, beloved, the words of Paul: "To the pure all things are pure, but to those who are defiled and unbelieving nothing is pure" (Titus 1:15). If the accuser has defiled us, then the way we perceive others will be defiled. If our heart is not pure, then we will attribute impure motives to those who have pure hearts.

Passing the Test

Remember Joseph. He suffered great harm from his brothers and from Potipher's household in Egypt. He refused to allow bitterness to master him. If he had allowed bitterness to master him, then he would have given in to Potipher's wife. The Lord fulfilled His promise to him after he passed the test.

Are you passing the test?

For example, let us say that you are going through financial difficulties. The utility and credit card companies are sending you bills and are threatening to discontinue your service and to turn you over to the bill collectors. During this time, you find yourself in a tempting situation. While shopping at a place of business, you decide to purchase an item that costs twenty dollars. You hand the cashier a fifty-dollar bill. The cashier mistakenly gives you forty dollars in change. You begin to entertain the thought of this cashier's ten-dollar mistake as being a "blessing" from God. You say to yourself, "After all that I have been through, surely I deserve this "blessing." The pressure is on and you allow the devil to cloud your mind with lies, thus keeping you from realizing that keeping the ten dollars is the same is stealing it. Instead, the devil lures you into compromising honesty and integrity by convincing you it is a blessing from God. You fail the test by keeping the extra ten dollars. What you thought was a blessing was a test of obedience. In this case, even though you failed, you still have a chance to return the money.

The true blessing of God will come only after we pass the test. *Our perception of the difficult circumstances that we face in this life will determine our ability to do so.* Are our hearts becoming softer or harder in the midst of our difficulties? Are we blaming the Lord and others, or are we taking full responsibility for our actions and state of heart? *To the degree that we become Christ-like, to that same degree will we fulfill our Kingdom destiny in this life.* We have God's *acceptance* through faith in the blood of Christ, but He only *endorses* tested and approved character.

Lastly, remember the passion and sufferings of our Lord:

"'Who committed no sin, nor was deceit found in His mouth' (23) who, when He was reviled, did not revile in return; when he suffered, He did not threaten, but committed Himself to Him who judges righteously; (24) who Himself bore our sins in His own body on the tree, that we, having died to sins, might live for righteousness – by whose stripes you were healed".

(1 Peter 2:22-24)

After Jesus endured such on our behalf, the Father said to Him, "Sit at my right hand, till I make Your enemies Your footstool" (Psalm 110:1). Jesus endured because He kept His eyes on the eternal reward set before Him. This gave Him the strength to finish His course in this life.

Prophecy:

"Who will entirely abandon themselves to a life of absolute trust in their God? If you knew Me as the One who judges righteously, you would fear no one except Me. Is it not written that all flesh is grass and its glory is as the flower of grass? The grass withers and the flower fades because the Wind of God blows upon it. I am sending a Wind that will cause the glory of flesh that is prevalent in My Church to wither. When that which you have gloried in is seen for what it really is, then to whom shall you turn? Then you will know Me as the only One to fear and the only One to absolutely trust. When you cease to glory in the withering flesh of men, when the unified cry of my people is "all flesh is as grass and its glory is as the flower of grass," then the way shall be made for My abiding glory in your midst. Then you shall see and know Me with a pure heart and the glory of your God shall arise upon you. You will recognize me through one another. Prepare the way of the Lord and make a straight path for Him to be revealed in your generation."

Truths in Review

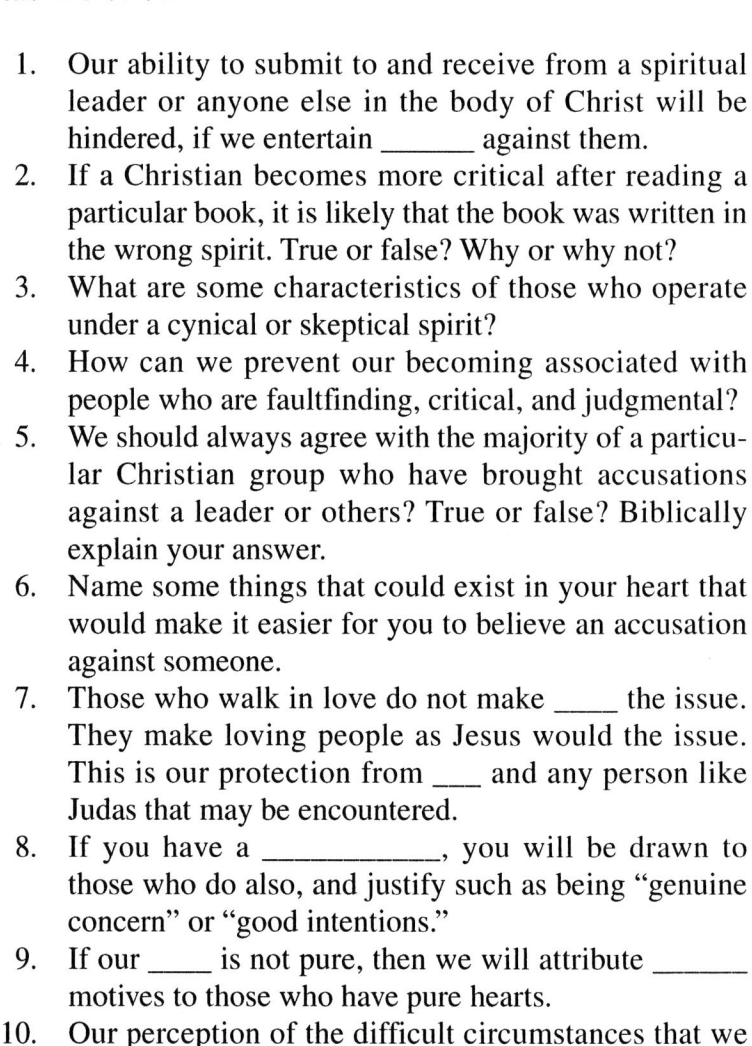

1. Our ability to submit to and receive from a spiritual leader or anyone else in the body of Christ will be hindered, if we entertain _____ against them.
2. If a Christian becomes more critical after reading a particular book, it is likely that the book was written in the wrong spirit. True or false? Why or why not?
3. What are some characteristics of those who operate under a cynical or skeptical spirit?
4. How can we prevent our becoming associated with people who are faultfinding, critical, and judgmental?
5. We should always agree with the majority of a particular Christian group who have brought accusations against a leader or others? True or false? Biblically explain your answer.
6. Name some things that could exist in your heart that would make it easier for you to believe an accusation against someone.
7. Those who walk in love do not make ____ the issue. They make loving people as Jesus would the issue. This is our protection from ___ and any person like Judas that may be encountered.
8. If you have a _____, you will be drawn to those who do also, and justify such as being "genuine concern" or "good intentions."
9. If our ____ is not pure, then we will attribute _____ motives to those who have pure hearts.
10. Our perception of the difficult circumstances that we face in this life will determine our ability to pass God's tests. True or false? Why or why not?.

The Conclusion

"Now when He was in Jerusalem at the Passover, during the feast, many believed in His name when they saw the signs which He did. (24) But Jesus did not commit Himself to them, because He knew *all* men, (25) and had no need that anyone should testify of man, for He knew what was in man".

(John 2:23-25; italics mine)

Like Jesus, we must know what is in man. When we rightly look into man's glory, we will see that all flesh is grass and the glory thereof as the flower of grass (Isaiah 40:6-8). We must know, deep in our heart, that the basis for our identity and destiny is not found in him—in that which is withering away. This knowledge of man is achieved by our allowing God's truth to first reveal what is in us (Matthew 7:1-5), and is imperative to our becoming overcomers in every sphere of life.

The word "commit" in the above passage of Scripture is defined: "to think to be true, to be persuaded of, to credit, place confidence in." Philippians 3:3 proclaims: "For we are the circumcision, who worship God in the Spirit, rejoice in Christ Jesus, and have NO confidence in the flesh" (emphasis mine). Fallen humanity cannot be accredited with anything that is true and cannot be trusted on any level as far as God is concerned. Even those who are mature in Christ have an element of darkness in them. "God is light and in Him is no darkness at all" (1 John 1:5). This statement, from the Apostle John, is made only about God to the exclusion of everyone else.

Even those who we might laud as awesome spiritual leaders have the potential to fail, disappoint, offend, wound, and neglect us. They all at some point will not meet our expectations. Then, to whom should we primarily direct our expectations? Who can we trust? The answer: the Father of lights with whom there is no variation or shadow of turning (James 1:17). He never changes and is rich to all who call on Him (Roman 10:12).

> In Roman 10:6-9, Paul reveals:
> "But the righteousness of faith speaks in this way, 'Do not say in your heart, who will ascend into heaven?' (that is, to bring Christ down *from above*) (7) or, 'who will descend into the abyss?' (that is, to bring Christ up from the dead). (8) But what does it say? 'The word is near you, in your mouth and in your heart' (that is, the word of faith which we preach): (9) that if you confess with your mouth the Lord Jesus and believe in your heart that God has raised Him from the dead, you will be saved".
>
> (Romans 10:6-9)

The word of God is the window by which we peer into the Kingdom of God and know (see) the realities of all the unseen treasures available to us in Christ. Faith involves being able to see and lay hold with our hearts these things and cooperate with the Lord in bringing them to pass in this realm. Without this ability to look into the Eternal, we would be without hope in this life. Our ability to maintain this eternal perspective throughout our sojourn in this life will be directly proportional to the purity of our heart. We will either lay hold of the unshakable realities of the Eternal or find unstable, temporary substitutes in this life.

Will you look into that "Presence behind the veil" that only the blood of Christ can give boldness to face and purity of heart to see? As we steadfastly look into the glory of God through His

The Conclusion

word as revealed through the cross of Christ, our search for healing, acceptance, self-worth, security, intimacy, dignity, honor, and love will end. Our soul will find its rest under the ruling authority of Him whose yoke is easy and burden light. We will realize the hope that is an anchor of our soul that is both sure and steadfast, and enters the "Presence behind the veil."

The restless soul of a Christian is the workshop of the deceiver. The restless soul looks away from the All Sufficient One with an unbelieving heart to find fulfillment in what is passing away. Will we as God's people look into His magnificence and splendor and realize that Heaven and earth are filled with His glory and that the glory of all flesh is as the withering flowers of the field?

Along with Jesus, we can know what is in all people, both good and evil, no matter how it appears outwardly, and know that God is all in all.

May we be found with our spiritual eyes fixed on that for which we have already received a down payment. When that which is Perfect comes, then that which is dim and in part will be swept away as we look into the Glory that shall be revealed. Our deepest longing for God, that has only found expression through groaning, will find consummation in the countenance of Him whose eyes are as a flame of fire—eyes from which *nothing* is hidden.

Father, deliver us from the pain that makes us self-absorbed, and the unbelief that keeps us looking to people for what we can only get from You. Deliver us from the resulting pride that seeks other means besides the cross to regain the sense of dignity that we have lost because of sin. Deliver us with from our obsession with ourselves—our pain, self-loathing, "successes," and goodness. Purify our hearts, oh God! We want to see You as You are and all flesh as they are. We want to love as You love. In Jesus' most excellent name, we pray. Amen.

Little children, keep your hearts pure and cultivate your love for the Truth until He comes. May He find us looking with Heaven's eyes and following the witness of His Spirit in our hearts. Amen.

THE END